Barbara Grossly

Books by Geoffrey Wolff

Bad Debts
The Sightseer
Black Sun: The Brief Transit and Violent Eclipse of Harry Crosby
Inklings

Geoffrey Wolff

Random House
New York

Library of Congress Cataloging in Publication Data

Wolff, Geoffrey, 1937–
Inklings.

I. Title.
PZ4.W8568In   1978   [PS3573.053]   813'.5'4   77–5988
ISBN 0–394–49349–4

Manufactured in the United States of America
2 4 6 8 9 7 5 3
First Edition

Design by Anne Lian

For Priscilla

[A little book] fits easily in the pocket, can be carried every-where, ready to give life and hope—in fact, the opposite of a revolver.

—Jean Cocteau

'Twas not by ideas—by Heaven; his life was put in jeopardy by words.

—Laurence Sterne, *Tristram Shandy*

Words are loaded pistols.

—Jean-Paul Sartre

Contents

Part One
MISCHIEF

My name is Jupe, and Jupe is what I'm called. I'm of a certain age, I'm forty-five. This morning I ate a bully English breakfast and went downstairs to my study. I live in New York, near Gramercy Park, and my study is below street level. I had no plans, I meant to read something substantial, I wasn't sure what; I heard the mail fall against my door, and I opened the door and tripped against a couple of publishers' review copies. I couldn't see them: perhaps I'm going blind, perhaps I don't try hard enough to see. I picked up one of the book packages and cut my finger on a staple holding it shut. I tore at it, and mouse-nest stuffing leaked from between its layers and stuck to my shirt. Inside was a first novel; the publisher wanted my opinion. According to the rules, if I read it to its conclusion it was a *masterpiece;* an *enduring* book was bound by cloth and boards, and *ephemeral* meant *unpublished.* I bled on the novel, which was perhaps a good novel, and dropped it in my rubbish basket, and sucked my bleeding finger. I reminded myself that I was self-indulgent, and felt sorry for myself that I continued to feel sorry for myself.

I read letters, holding them to the light, inches from my eyes. North American University, with its campus in an Arizona post-office box, announced, again, that it was privileged to offer me its Honorary Doctorate of Letters come June: no need to pick the thing up there, they'd send it along, $200, for postage, handling, and printing, framing could be arranged. *Who's Who in the East* wondered whether it was possible that throughout yet another year there had been no improvement in my situation, nothing to add to my attainments. Were they thinking of dropping me? A tit magazine—*Hombre!*—propositioned me:

> We are asking a number of persons distinguished in the worlds of sport and fashion, politics and theater, media and the arts—men thought about by men—to write their obituaries. We will pay an honorarium of $50 on submission and $250 on publication. Pieces should be short (100–150 words), muscular, and light. Like you, we are interested in having fun.
>
> The Editor: *Hombre!*

Reflexively, I balled the form letter and dumped it into the trash. But then I retrieved it, smoothed it flat, took it to my typewriter and banged out my memorial notice:

> Born in Seattle, raised here and there. Schooled at Oxford. Taught Modern Literature, till all the moderns died. First book published at 30. More followed, riding the backs of other people's creations. Books about fictions, and fictioneers. Turned sour. Considered by enemies a rogue critic, running amok among hymn-singers, toad-

ies, trimmers, and muse-fuckers. Considered by friends to have been rigorous, and to be now as enemies have always perceived me. Only recently began to think in terms of enemies and friends. Happily married. For seven years a father: in place of a minor novel made a major child, a thing likely to outlive your correspondent. Who wished only one thing before he died, a secret wish: to write his novel. Who died without having written his novel.

Well, it wasn't "light," and it wasn't much fun. But it was more than 100 and less than 150 words, they could count on me to write to space.

My desk was a battlefield: a letter from my lawyer telling me I could avoid a court appearance after all in the matter of a malicious mischief charge two weeks back (I had defaced a bust of Sir Walter Scott in the Ramble of Central Park), and a letter from a novelist I had abused in print for having dared an authorial intrusion upon a third-person narrative. I had, I conceded, condemned him excessively, and now I condemned him excessively for having complained of his treatment. For months now I had been picking fights, deflating reputations, flunking students, boxing the ears of credit managers who dunned me, whose bills I left unpaid precisely to provoke them to dun me so that I could scrap with them.

Why so prickly? An editor, once a friend, promised me a dime a word for an essay. The essay I delivered wasn't very good, but he printed it; he also miscounted it, and his check was shy $7.20. I accused him of treachery, called him a shyster, I'd never used the word till then, till last month. Why so nettlesome, why such a sourpuss justice-seeker? In part: I took recently to tracking down my books in open-stack libraries, to see who had charged them out; some had never been read, others had wisecracks scrawled in their margins, and no recent readers. In part: a recent survey of literary critics used its second printing to drop me from its index. In part: someone was following me around New York. In part: perhaps I was going blind.

It began with something palpable, a slight occlusion of vision in the corner of my left eye, near my nose. I felt it one morning, it caused a dry, uncertain blink, as though something needed lubrication. I could see it, I thought, before I saw it. In the mirror it looked like a purple mole, an unnecessary fold of horny skin. It might have been a bruise, and in class that afternoon at the university one of my students asked about it: "Hey, sir! Hey, who hung the mouse on your eye?" This week I threw a message over his wall, flunked him. The useless addition to my face has continued to swell, though not by much, and I imagine that it is merely the visible evidence of something deeply wrong with my senses—sight, smell, taste— and perhaps with my reason. I am afraid (see Hawthorne, "The Birthmark"). Today, when I had finished with my mail, I left my house, without telling Kate, and went to a doctor. The doctor was a stranger; I am private; Kate is my wife.

The eye doctor asked me what was the trouble. I thought his question was frivolous, and must have showed my contempt. We were not going to be friends, I thought; I thought that what friends I would have in life I already had.

"My eyes are the trouble." The doctor stared at me, said nothing. "I can't see clearly. When I read I don't concentrate anymore. Reading is my profession. That is, I read."

The doctor did not say *I see,* as I thought he would. He said "I understand."

"Yes, well, now I'm rationing books. Perhaps it will seem silly, but I think of my sight as a pistol with only a few rounds left loaded. I don't want to waste them. Junk mail angers me."

The doctor did not say, as I thought he would, *You have come to the wrong kind of doctor, you should see a psychiatrist.* The doctor instead said "You perhaps need glasses."

I tried to interest the doctor in a paper I had written at Oxford and had tried the night before to read. About Oedipus and Lear, sight imagery, obsessive, grim stuff about "orbs" and "spectacles" and vital jelly and spies and blindness and seers . . .

"Perhaps you need glasses?"

I submitted to his tests. The doctor was indifferent to the unsightly pouch of unnatural flesh that hung in the corner of my eye. He agreed that it was not attractive, but insisted that it caused me to remind him of Franklin Roosevelt, whom his mother (but not his father) had held in highest esteem. The tests were inconclusive. As he shifted lenses in front of a binocular device, I did indeed sense a distinction between letters that were blurred and letters that were not. But as these letters spelled nothing, or spelled nothing that was of interest to me, I would not, indeed could not, discriminate between displeasing sensations. The doctor, a patient man, nevertheless suggested that I return to try again.

"Glasses aren't so bad," he said. "I wear them."

"Yes," I said, "you do."

"They make me look bookish, my wife tells me."

"I wouldn't say so," I said.

"They aren't the end of the world," he said.

"No, they aren't."

"People won't tease you, call you four-eyes."

"I'm certain that they won't."

"Well," he said. "Well?"

"Thank you," I said, and paid him, and left.

I like to recall myself sitting a few hours later across a table from Fugelman. He made me look good. A squirt, sawing the air like the circus master in *The Travels of Babar,* trying to catch a waiter's eye. We were in the lobby of the Algonquin. He would moan, "Damn, I need a drink," and clear his throat as though a bone were stuck in it, but no one noticed. He would ring the service bell on our table. The bell was bolted to the table. Fugelman would bang on it, and no one would come.

I sat still. There wasn't room enough beneath the low table for my range-master's legs, so I tucked them beneath my chair. (My physical discomfort there was only one of many reasons I tried to keep clear of the Algonquin.) I watched Fugelman work himself up to the edge of hysteria, and then I jerked my head to toss some hair out of my eyes. Bang—a waiter flew to my side. I nodded to Fugelman: "You order first."

He began a windy program of instruction for the fabrication of his martini. "Silver bullet," he called it, "mart." I called it loudmouth soup. While Fugelman demanded, and modified his demands, the waiter wrote nothing down. Presently he cut my companion's speech off and turned to me.

"Buttermilk. Please."

"We have no buttermilk, I think. We have skimmed. I think."

"No thank you. No buttermilk, nothing."

"I understand. Sir." He went off nodding his head, approving: in the library of my desires, no shelf space for compromise, and in my perhaps idealized version of the little drama the waiter respected that.

While Fugelman jabbered, waving his hands like an Italian tenor, I listened, peering across the steeple I had made with my fingers, pretending to look at him gravely, to see him as he saw himself. I'd nod, I'd shake my head, I'd recoil when he reached out to touch my arm. Sometimes I'd speak:

"My price is my price. Pay and I'll deliver. Otherwise make yourself—that's a nice figure of speech we use, no? *make yourself*—another deal."

Fugelman didn't need me. But he didn't know he didn't need me. I knew it, and I tapped my breast pocket to feel my pen, just in case he sprung a contract on me. A theater party of matrons at the next table nodded in unison. They'd been eavesdropping: they got it—under my cavalry twill I wore a snub-nose in a breakaway holster. My God, it was their first, a bona-fide button man contracting a hit not twenty feet from the Round Table. In a way, given what came after, I guess they were seeing what they thought they were seeing.

"Okay, Jupe. Jesus. I'll play. But don't think you're all that special. Four hundred apiece for your goons, half a grand for you. But you've got to take Scharmon."

"Who needs him? He's a jerk, what's in it for him? He doesn't need the dough. What dough? Four hundred, nickels and dimes, shoo."

"He likes the action, I like him. Okay?"

"Okay. But I want Baby Hughie and Nick."

"What for? What's in it for them? They don't need the action."

"They need the dough."

"A deal. But don't screw up, I've been hearing stuff about you. You know? No mess, I'm not kidding, I want a clean job. You'll get the green when it's done. Agreed?"

I nodded.

"Shake," he said.

I let Fugelman hold my hand a few seconds, then stood up abruptly. My legs were asleep, but I limped outside and turned toward Fifth Avenue and the spring wind stood me right up straight. I maneuvered against the whiny gusts roaring through the canyon of 45th Street from the East River and made out a galleon of a black man driven downwind toward me. He was done up in red: sweater, socks, knit cap, all red. He was singing, more or less, at a bellow: *Oh what a beeyootifulll mornin, oh what a beeyooootifull day, I've got a beyoooootiful feeeeelin, everythins goan my way!* Sure. Tears ran down his cheeks: the wind worked against my eyes and tears ran down my cheeks. He was dippy, out of central casting for Black Comedy, put on earth to be shanghaied into a skinny novel described on its flyleaf as *extravagant . . . absurd . . . sick . . .* Sick. The black man's excess and the great noise of him reached me, and as we passed I pressed a bill into his pink palm, and he nodded and never lost the beat of his fortissimo prophecy: *Everythins goan my way!*

What was the hurry? I loitered in front of the Hammond showroom. At stage right of an improvised auditorium some huckster was at the keyboard of a Novachord, leading a dozen or so marks in a watery chorus of "Heartaches." They sat on foldaway chairs. I couldn't make out their faces, but they must have liked the guy's work because he was taking it from the top again. His hair was of cresting silver waves. Everyone must have suspected him of wearing a rug, but I had a hunch the awful waves were real; it must have been hard on him. He sat in the show window, three feet from my face. Beside him were visual aids, sandwich boards done in old-fashioned Day-Glo: "Do It, NOW!" "Sing, NOW!" "PLAY!" "Amaze." Shoo. What an age. People would only go if they could ride, by shortcut. I couldn't abide amateurs: if a man believed he could learn to make music in six weeks, we shouldn't let him play. We?

I pushed on faster, eager to be home. Half a block and then,

in front of the Harvard Club, something turned me around.
Just in time to squint at him disappearing into a doorway. My
shadow again! I wanted a showdown, and turned west toward
the Algonquin, but I felt a tug at my sleeve. I thought it was
the wind, the pull was so slight. But it was a guy with a cup,
bracing me. He wore a placard, slung from his neck by a piece
of clothesline: *Being Down On My Luck Help a Poor Poet Like
Me Like Get By. P.S. I GOT A SOAR THROAT!* I yanked
away my sleeve but the beggar, weak as he was, grabbed it
again, tugged again. A hungry look. Maybe a knife, even in
front of the Harvard Club?

"Gimme," he said.

"Pardon?" I said.

"Gimme bucks. I want to buy a notebook."

"I already gave. Just up the block. To the Negro singer."

"The what?"

"The singer."

"What singer?"

"The black man."

"What the fuck's that to me? Gimme a buck . . ."

He kept at me, jerking my sleeve with one hand and sticking
his cup at me with the other. So I gave up pulling and pushed,
and he let go, and his cup went flying. It wasn't tin at all, but
silver. Something the scribbler had been given on naming-day,
no doubt, long before his beaming mum and dad could have
imagined that he would translate himself from a human child
into a poet, a beggar. He sat on the sidewalk, rocking back and
forth, sweeping up the coins that I'd scattered. I made a move
to help him, but he swept me away, thought I might rob him.
I stood looking down, waiting to be excused.

"Hey, mister, everybody says 'fuck' these days. What's the
beef? Everybody says it . . ."

"But not to me."

"Okay, wow, leave me be. New York, what a city, all I did was ask for dough, you gotta ask don't you? You can't even talk to strangers anymore, ask for help, I'm a poet, times are bad . . ."

"When you stop your glottals, and unsplit your infinitives, and undangle your participles, and square away your spelling, send me a poem. Maybe I'll review it. Maybe I'll even pay for it. But now pick up your cup, and your money, and your sign, and fuck off."

"Okay, mister, wow, what's your name?"

"My name is Jupe, and I'm sorry I spilled your money."

And I want you to believe I was one raw, mean, businesslike hombre. I wanted my shadow to believe too. I couldn't see him. Maybe he wasn't even there anymore. Maybe he had never been there. Maybe he was there and couldn't see me. Tough conundrums for a tough guy. Shoo.

Home. I had lost my shadow, or he had lost me.

The Algonquin matrons would have been crushed. My place was no triggerman's hideout. Merely a regulation Gramercy Park duplex, most of its walls lined floor to ceiling with books printed in several languages and giving superficial evidence of having been read.

And she who stretched out her arms to greet me as though I had been gone days rather than hours? Kate, no moll, my wife, Kate. Her hair was thick, with a touch of red for temper. Her skin was pale. But she can take the sun, she's got iron in her, she can take it. Dish it out, too . . . I love her.

"What happened at the Algonquin? Did Fugelman do you, or did you do him?"

And I replayed it for her entertainment, did Fugelman's shrill voice and beat the air with my hands; I even screwed myself down into my chair, managing somehow to diminish myself. Kate clapped: she was always a generous audience. I told how Fugelman had moaned when I'd told him the subject of our symposium: *The Death of the Novel.* "It's been done, Jupe, it's been done . . . to death." Poor Fugelman, chairman of the program committee of the American chapter of Writers Inc., was obliged to schedule and book acts for the first convention ever in New York of the world-wide association of scribblers. And justly fearing for the security of his job he wanted the affair to come off sweetly and simply, no hitches, unpissed-in soup. He had arranged shopping expeditions for the conventioneers and a night at the Latin Quarter and a boat trip around Manhattan. Bright and Cheery was the motif. Till this, *The Death of the Novel.* Whoa! Bad enough it was a snore of a topic; worse, it might be controversial, people, some people, had strong feelings about death.

Poets, essayists, novelists, reviewers—six hundred pen-persons from eighty countries—were due in town the Friday of Memorial Day weekend to give one another prizes, to make enemies of one another, drone at one another about the crisis of translation, the crisis of technology, the crisis of concrete verse, of the *école du regard,* of copyright . . . Every year they traveled, on their taxpayers' magic carpets, to present some manifesto *(Free the Basques! Free Harry Reems! Free verse!),* buy duty-free Jack Daniel's, and get a topless shoeshine. And every year fights broke out: between the Turks and the Greeks, between the Ugandans and the Kenyans, between the Israelis and half the world, between the Americans and the other half. For the drudges obliged to organize these conventions, who took the rap for bloodshed, the carnage was awful, the job expectancy short. So Fugelman was beside himself with anxiety.

For he had decided that *his* convention, by God, would be remembered till the end of time for its amicability. And he had chosen me to master the intellectual ceremonies at the climactic Saturday meeting because I spoke softly, and had what he called "a nice clean accent—neutral, you know?" And because the poet scheduled to read to the audience, and lull it, was boycotting the convention. Someone, his friend or enemy, had not got, had got, a Writers Inc. prize, or something. So now, two days before the convention, I had sprung this topic on him, and threatened to link the beastliness of novelists with the moribundity of their form, had said I might raise the matter of politics if it suited me. Fugelman could see it all: a hotheaded Mexican fictioneer would lead his delegation from the hall, the communists would blame the fascists for the inaccessibility of modern letters, the Spanish would abuse the Bulgarians, the newspapers would crack wise the next day, Fugelman would lose another job. No: he wouldn't have it. How about something nice: *The New Journalism: Whither and Whether?*

"How did you bring him around, Jupe?"

"I suggested a couple of alternatives: *Literature and the Murder of Allende* and *Art as Mediator Between Feminism and the Gay Liberation Front.* Trendy, no? He suggested something on the *Problems of Translation* and I told him the newspaper people would stay home in their hundreds. He said they'd stay home from my own topic, and I agreed with him. He liked that. Said 'What the hell, no one else raises his voice these days, why shouldn't we? Let's take a position, the old here-I-stand-I-can-do-no-other razzmatazz. If the novel's dead, let's tell 'em so, who cares anyway?' Also, there are conditions."

"No money? Say it ain't so, Jupe."

"A little money. But I've got to ask Scharmon to speak."

"But why would that whiner want to join a symposium on —Lord!—*The Death of the Novel?*"

"Why indeed? Fugelman says he likes the billing. Fugelman's got a point. The only way to keep your name before the public is to make a public asshole of yourself, the more often and the more public the better. Scharmon likes ink, I guess. I shoved Nick and Baby Hughie down Fugelman's throat."

"Why Baby Hughie?"

"We were friends. We liked each other, and I'd like us to like each other again."

"You're not realistic, Jupe."

"I waste too much time hanging around realism, indulge me."

"What else happened?"

"There are ground rules, Fugelman's code of symposium etiquette."

"Let me guess," Kate said. "You aren't to mention the name of a living writer whose work you don't admire."

"Right."

"You are not to single out any nation or political system as being more responsible than any other nation or political system for the death of the what's-its-name?"

"Right."

"You are to fly from controversy, remembering that every question, like every iron curtain, has two sides; you will be courteous always, and you won't get paid if you fuck up."

"Bingo!"

"You're a genius, Jupe."

Genius? Kate would only pronounce the word ironically; I wouldn't have used it at all, for any reason. By my lights I was a critic, a pretty good one. I took responsibility for a book every couple of years—the kind that develops from seminars on *The Life of the Novel*—and I taught at the university and made pin money from a steady course of book reviews. I was said to write lucidly, used question marks seldom and exclamation points less than seldom. I took satisfaction from meeting deadlines: I was a pro—my proudest claim—I kept promises. I had never violated my integrity, but then nobody had ever asked me to violate it. My name used to appear on some lists of New York Intellectuals (the rubric made me wince, but see me wince now that I'm left off), the rosters published every month or so in *The New York Times Magazine*. In other words, on the face of it, I was a dime a dozen.

But not to Fugelman. Why? Because I was born and raised in the Pacific Northwest, out there beyond the Pillars of Hercules where the literary wars between the Village and the Upper West Side are not even a dim memory. I was a noncombatant, and just as I was unencumbered by any recognized geo-cultural baggage, so was I ethnically *tabula rasa:* non-black, non-Jew, non-Nordic, unattached. I was not even thought of as a WASP. Despite three years at Oxford I managed to treat all characters of the alphabet equally under the laws of pronunciation. Fugelman liked a few others of what he thought of as my virtues: I went seldom to Elaine's, I refused without discrimination to write dust-jacket plugs, and to sign petitions, and to give money to free pornographers from prisons. So I had had, till recently, few public enemies.

Merely a private one.

"Kate, the son of a bitch followed me again, he picked up my tail when I left Fugelman at the Algonquin."

She had the grace not to smirk, but she winked when she asked "What does he look like?"

She didn't take me seriously. What *did* he look like? I had no eye for faces, had no eyes for much of anything these days, but I could mimic the merest stranger's voice. I could give an account of his clothes: army-issue khaki trousers, a bush jacket bristling with attachments. And he had fair hair, cut close. His shadow had fallen across me often that winter and spring, on the lecture circuit, in the corridor outside my classroom, in the Reading Room of the big library on Fifth and Forty-second, in the Gotham Book Mart, at the Y. And only the night before, though I did not tell Kate this, I had thought I saw a face— gaunt, needful, disappointed, familiar, most familiar—through the pane of my study window. I had even dreamt of the character, and in my dream my antagonist was a construct of letters, come to life from a bowl of cold alphabet soup. But I managed to discount this dream, together with all my dreams. It was such a commonplace nightmare, and I knew too well how to decode it. It came not from a midnight feast of oysters but from a midnight dose of Contemporary Literature populated with golems and doppelgangers.

"Oh," I answered, "he looks like a writer, I guess, just a novelist."

"Well, there you are! He's probably trying to put the arm on you for a review."

"You're probably right," I told Kate, thinking she was probably wrong.

"I had a run-in with a guy today, shoved him, wanted to hit him. A beggar pretending to be a poet, or a poet disguised as a beggar, I can't tell the difference, I had murder in my heart."

"Oh, Jupe. *Why?*"

She asked why; she would. She asked questions because she believed in answers, and usually she got them. But there was no rational reply to that *why*. I might have confessed that my coarse duel with Fugelman had debased rather than entertained me. I could have told her that I was losing my sight, but I wouldn't tell her that, and I didn't know whether I believed it anyway. I could have told her that I wished I had written a novel, but to that she would have asked an even more intimidating WHY?

"Jupe? Will you answer me? What did the beggar do to you? Why so angry?"

"He was rude to me."

"Oh, for God's sake, everyone's rude to everyone."

"He cursed me."

"Everyone curses . . ."

"Ungrammatically."

"Ah," Kate said, beginning to comprehend. "Nevertheless . . ."

But that was all: in ran Robin, our little boy, at full charge. He tried to hug us both at once, and was spilling adventure yarns, the day's doings. When he was done with his dramatizations he stood below me where I stood, and looked up from far down.

"Tell me a story."

And Kate said, "Daddy doesn't *tell* stories, dear, he doesn't make them up. He reads stories, remember?"

And the boy, still looking up at me—for confirmation?—got a crooked smile; no story, just an odd, frosty grin.

3

Nick was my friend, Nick the Novelist. You used to find his name on lists of comers, never at the lead-off spot, but never at the bottom of the roster, either. His first novel was reviewed on the cover of the same *New York Times Book Review* that sent my first study of the novel to the back of the bus. But his first was also his last, and a long time had passed since then. Nick was a grudging writer, grudging talker, too. He was on record as believing that most short stories were too long: *If you can't make a metaphor do its work in a couple of thousand words, find another metaphor, or another line of work.*

Readers honored him for his taciturnity, and his splendid book went mostly unread, which was all right with him, he was no pusher. He'd do the odd job in the odd classroom, commit a story to print, rustle up food and shelter. He had been married to a good lady, and she died. Except for poking a dancer from some rub joint now and again, he was without evident weaknesses, a serious man. He had consequence, my friend, was in bondage only to the just trope.

Because I was a critic, and often a reviewer, he was also my friendly foe. He called my work "chatterbox stuff," and professed astonishment that anyone could, that anyone would, write to order and to measure and to an editor's schedule. I did not feel that he scorned me or my work, only that it baffled him. Like generals of opposing Civil War armies who were once roommates at the same service academy, we shared a canon of mental behavior and what we were pleased to regard as a code of honor.

Now, the day before the symposium, I was trying to rope Nick into my little mob, because I liked him and because I knew he needed four hundred dollars. I hoped he would agree to join me, if only for whatever it is that calls one celebrated gunslinger into a street showdown with his quickest rival, but in this hope I betrayed too high an opinion of my own speed, celebrity, and weight.

"Well," said Nick. "One-on-one. Wanna fight?"

"I never fight at home. We'd wake Kate." I didn't smile, didn't even shake my head.

"You've got no business hanging out with feebs and bumble-puppies," Nick said to me. "I've told you before. Why are you doing this?"

"Fugelman asked me to."

"Bullshit! You're going anarchic on me. Why?"

"Because most days I can't get my pen up. I can only get it up for whores."

"Someone called you a literary gangster the other day, and I laughed. Hell, I've known you a long time, and I've never thought of you that way. But now I don't know. You've written some spiteful stuff lately, you've been acting like a shark, I hear things. Maybe if you kept better company you wouldn't get so angry all the time."

"Nick, Nick, Nick, you've got it backwards. I'm a sheriff, pal, shoring up standards, mending loose talk, restoring 'presently' to its proper usage, keeping jerks in line . . ."

"They aren't all jerks, you know."

"I know. I guess I know. But, Jesus Christ, the times are bad: some skin magazine just asked me to write my own obit on spec, and instructed me to *make it cute.*"

"I got the letter. Who didn't? I didn't read it through, why did you?"

"I answered it."

"Jesus, Jupe."

"But doesn't it piss you off that the only writers who hit lucky numbers are the ones who cheat, lazy bastards willing to score off current events, or someone else's bad luck? Think of the bullshit people buy: fictions about the high spiritual energy of a seagull, for Christ's sake, about . . . about . . ."

"What has that got to do with me? What has it got to do with you? What's Scharmon got to do with you? Baby Hughie?"

"One of them used to be a friend. The other was . . . pressed upon me."

"Baby Hughie isn't of your tribe. Why not leave him be. What do you mean Scharmon was 'pressed' upon you?"

"Fugelman made me take him on."

"Made you? What *made* you? You don't have to do the goddamned symposium at all."

"Neither do you. Besides, my colleagues represent to me the Truth of Our Times. They are . . . them. Understand?"

"I understand you're in trouble. If you believe your choices have been reduced to a single choice between solitude and the company of grifters . . ."

"That's enough, Nick. Don't worry about me, and I won't worry about you."

"I had sort of hoped that you—in the role of my friend, understand—would worry about me."

"Hey, this is too heavy, we're too frail to bear freight like this."

Then we drank milk together, and I managed to make Nick smile. I told him my notion of a different, more generous kind of National Book Award ceremony, something akin to the annual Kennedy Pet Show, at which every animal won a first prize. There would be awards for The Best Biography of a Man Born on June 2, 1898; and for The Best Novel Titled *Love Story*. The Best Likeness on a Dust-Jacket Photograph would win a blue ribbon, and so would The Best Job of Spelling. Everybody would be happy. But Nick was not happy. He was not happy with me. He stared at me. I blinked, looked at the rug. He made going-home noises. I begged him to stay, talk, have another drink.

"You're down on your ass, Jupe."

"I guess."

Nick talked about some of my recent fractious provocations. Said I was making of my career a beggar's crossroad, a gravedigger's scorecard. Said I put him in mind of some comic actor the jaded rich used to hire for formal dinner parties. This was back in the twenties, and Nick couldn't recollect the actor's name, "His celebrity died with his act." His gimmick was to masquerade as a waiter, and then insult the unknowing guests; only the host knew what was what. The waiter would dump soup in the guests' laps, or smother the beef Wellington in ketchup, or stack dishes up his arm like a short-order busboy when he cleared the table. He might snip a few inches off a man's necktie with a pair of pruning shears. The guests would complain to the host and he would shrug and say, "What can I do? Can't get decent help nowadays." A funny act, till everyone got to be a wised-up host, and there weren't any suckers left. "Jupe, you remind me of that joker . . ."

"Who's laughing?"

"Oh, you used to, used to laugh a lot. But now you're getting squeezed by the new realities. Everyone's a knowing host these days, everyone knows everything that doesn't matter. And you keep cranking out stunts, each wilder than the last. Some of them are funny, to people who don't care about you. But everyone's catching the drift of the play. Of course you are also a talented servant, decent help, quite rare, and we creative employers appreciate you, don't think we're indifferent to your gifts. Deep, clear water, Jupe, but too cold. You're tart, short on mercy. You used to be just . . ."

"When I was a kid I won the Seattle spelling bee. Got to the final round of the Northwest Regionals. The last word I spelled correctly was 'clement,' an easy one. I got beaten by three syllables, 'rig-or-ous.' A silly mistake. I never forgave myself for having committed it."

"That's what we creative writers call a *conceit*, Jupe. We're talking real . . ."

"Don't lecture me on lies, novelist."

"Day's done, I'm going home."

"To work?"

"To work."

"Will I see you in court tomorrow, Counsellor?"

"No, you won't."

"I didn't think so. I'm sorry."

"I'm sorry, too, Jupe, but not about that."

"I know."

"No, you don't. You did, but you don't."

Well, at least I'd make mischief in the morning, make it hot for the fictioneers. Literary gangster, my ass. Maybe I was apostate. Maybe. Was I a literary gangster because I denied the sanctity of the lies people were pleased to call fictions? What was a fiction, after all? A conjurer's cheap prestidigitation, no more than jiggery-pokery, moon-fluff, not to be weighed in earnest. "Not recommended," the *Consumer's Union* of intelligence would conclude tomorrow. Not that there were many consumers left to be warned off.

And as to that grand inner life, the miracle of creation that drove blurbists to their knees, causing them to see signs and speak in tongues and kiss the Novelist's hem: horseshit. What was this mystery of invention, after all? What children do at play, feigning ghosts and goblins, trying on fright masks, toying? What were novelists, after all, but kids tricked out as prophets and *provocateurs?* Fiction: insulting to laws of supply and demand—there was so much of it and so few cared. Why, then, did I so want to make it? The novel deserved to die. So why would it not die, and leave me in peace? Why, it might as well have asked, would I not die and leave it be?

And there was Kate, who knew me through and through. Her face was scrubbed and dry, and her color was high, as though she had been sitting near a fire. Nick's last words had wakened her, but her eyes were alive. Taken from deep sleep, she would come to the surface alert, all her sensing instruments —compass, thermometer, gyroscope—at full efficiency.

I was sitting cross-legged on the rug, my books stacked in front of me. I knew her opinion of them, though she thought it was her only secret from me. She liked best the first one, a

bluff and innocent appreciation, filled with eccentric enthusiasms for fictional odds and ends, for Albert Payson Terhune and Malcolm Lowry and P.G. Wodehouse. *Another,
Better World* I had called it. Well . . . *Titans*—may the god
of proportion forgive me—came next, a learned study of Mel-
ville, Hawthorne, James and Faulkner, the senior trustees. It
sewed up my teaching career, but Kate felt no affection for it.
Then I had edited an anthology of short novels, but it had
never been much in demand because my enthusiasm for my
own selections was under such evident control. Kate's inclina-
tions closely corresponded with mine in fiction, then, so she
liked the anthology, but we had never discussed my temperate
introductions and notes. Then came *Rereadings,* a sour
reevaluation of the same writers I had most admired in my first
book. Finally, *Who Says?* Finally and least loved. Who would
blame Kate? Despite me, against my wishes and my wits, my
study of contemporary fiction had degenerated into a diatribe
against living writers which seemed to seek to prove their
corporate creative inferiority to one living critic. An inferiority
of manner, learning, majesty and morality. Kate had said something kind about its energy, but we both knew that it was an
energy of bluster, that I had raised a sweat flailing with a
bastinado, an exertion damaging to the heart. What a declin-
ing arc did those books describe! From muse-struck boy to
measured judge to bully to envious bully. I felt chastened. And
by her expression, looking at my books stacked like wastepaper
to be chucked away, she said I should be chastened.

"Nothing to be ashamed of. Is there, Jupe?"

"No, of course not. I was just thinking, just wondering, what
would come next."

She didn't ask me what I planned to write next. She never
asked, because she had never believed I wanted her to ask. She

had thought my work was my secret, and from misbegotten habits of dignity and reserve I had neglected to tell her how much I wished her to ask what I would do next. Instead, without variation, every summer, soon after Independence Day, we went to our place in Maine. Odd-year summers I'd read, prepare for the next book behind the shut library door. Even-year summers I'd write, working smoothly, moving ahead unworried whether it would get done, worried only whether it mattered that it got done. One thousand words a day, written with evident good temper.

When the first one was finished I had given the typescript to Kate, and she had read it as though it were her own work, isolating errors and infelicities, never dreaming that she should play me delicately, worry about wounding me. With that book we had had the illusion of shared candor. Strike that: we had the reality of shared candor. But I no longer showed my work to Kate before it was published. I tried too hard to decode her *real* attitude toward my work, while she took offense at my assumption that there was a lacuna between her expressed and her authentic opinion of it. There was a lacuna . . .

"You're a fine critic, Jupe. You know that, don't you?"

I said nothing. I despised myself for the part I was playing: sulky, coy, delicately wounded. I wanted to come home to myself, but I couldn't find my way.

"What's the matter. Did that man follow you again?"

"Yes. I doubled back on him after he picked me up leaving class, and I caught him. I'm sure I know him from somewhere, asked him what the hell he wants from me. He shrugged . . ."

"The way you always shrug these days?"

I shrugged. "I guess so. He said 'Nothing, nothing.' He was carrying a little black account book, as though he might be The

Croaker himself, come to sign me up. I asked him if I could help him. He said 'No, sir, I don't think so, not now, maybe later.' So I asked him straight out, was he following me? And he said 'Just going your way, no harm, is there?' And walked away. To tell you the truth I feel lonely without him, I know him from somewhere, he frightens me, I don't know what I think, I think I'm going blind."

"Jupe, Jupe, Jupe. You need glasses, that's all. Go to a doctor."

"I already have gone."

"What did he tell you?"

"That I need glasses."

"Get them."

"I ordered them today. I just said, just brought you the news, that I'm going blind, that I think I'm going blind. You seem to take the intelligence stoically."

"I don't believe it. That's not your trouble."

"Tell me, then, what's my trouble?"

"You're worried about tomorrow?" I shook my head. "You won't do anything . . . silly?"

"When have I done anything silly?"

"Last week, when you went to the reception after Bellow's reading got up in that absurd gear . . ."

"Scandalous isn't silly . . ."

"*Silly*, dammit. A false nose is silly, a clip-on mustache is silly, a plastic spider on your lapel is silly, a squirting flower in your buttonhole, a joy buzzer, *silly!*"

"I won't argue with you."

"Is your new book troubling you? Tell me. If you want to. Please tell me."

I made, may Kate forgive me, a dismissing gesture with my hand, as though I had no wish to discuss it.

She was angry. "Well, *what* then?"

"Nothing, everything: it's all at the level of a literary cliché, don't mind me, I don't pity myself."

Kate tried a smile. "Be a good boy tomorrow, we can use the dough. You're tired, come to bed with me."

I said no, said I wanted to read.

"Not bad for a blind man." I didn't smile. She begged: "Please come, please rest, come with me, baby."

I stood up slowly. I was furious, not at her, just furious. "Goddammit, call me *mister*, call me *professor*, call me *hack*. But never, never, never call me *baby!* Okay?"

Kate, scorched, stood astounded. I thought I would weep. I didn't want any longer to be who I was. She read me for a couple of seconds, squinting. And finding there at length a story she knew, and was willing perhaps to like, she laughed. And I, till then holding my breath, let go in my own laughter. And together we went to bed.

Next morning we three wise men—keepers of culture's keys and bareback riders of the sedentary arts—prepared to turn our trick. We sat at an oval table to the left of a lectern, center stage, looking down at the ballroom of the Hotel LePage and at many rows of folding chairs. It was intellection day in global village, and on our table were the usual props of deep public thought: ashtrays, a nickel-plate water pitcher, index cards, books written by Germans.

The lights of an educational network's television crew blasted down on us from the balcony, raising our sweat and blinding me to the five or six hundred in the audience. We chatted with one another with practiced ease, feigning nonchalance for the United Nations of literary bureaucrats I had obliged myself to entertain. They stared at us without malice or curiosity, as though we were houseflies in a bottle.

Scharmon was the heavy, the one we loved to hate. His self-esteem was so invincible that he filed under "Miscellaneous Correspondence" carbon copies of the obscene mash notes he had written to his neighbor's wife. How do I know this? He's forthcoming, his trade is in confessions. For thirteen years Scharmon had confessed to his analyst, or tried to. That graybearded worthy preferred to discuss how much he was owed, and to drum up schemes that would put his windbag patient in the green. He managed to persuade Scharmon that he would never truly enjoy a piece of ass till he took responsibility for his debts. Perhaps his car could be sold? No good: it was in title to Scharmon's ex-wife, who had had the wit to take up with an accountant rather than a quack. The furniture? Ditto. There was a novel in Scharmon's works, of course, there was a novel in everyone's works, but no plugged nickel would come of it, this man wasn't an analyst for nothing. (Of course, that was the problem: he had been Scharmon's analyst for precisely nothing.)

One day, according to the legend, he was listening to his analysand bellyache about the exactions of mortality and the fickleness of fame, and while he nodded sagaciously at trumped-up dreams salted with swords and toppling towers and derailed trains and tree-rimmed swamps it came to him— *Eureka!* Why not a tell-all memoir? The doctor reasoned thus: since his patient's complaints were trivial and fundamentally indecent (one day he had looked across his desk at Scharmon, balled up a piece of scrap paper and thrown it at the wretched man, saying "You're not sick, you're rotten!"), they could be put to the use of elevating the self-regard of the generality of readers cast down by more noble sadnesses. By contrast to Scharmon's, the common reader's common misery would loom, he would feel more exquisitely the pain he suffered from the nips of life's fleas, he would feel enhanced, would broadcast his improvement to friends similarly afflicted, his friends would buy, Scharmon would grow rich and pay his bills and go away.

To shinny the greasy pole of best-seller lists Scharmon exploited his most useful assets: he was without shame or pride, would betray any confidence, would stoop to gossip, kiss-and-tell, not-kiss-but-tell-anyway. His ex-wife's kinky sense of fun appealed to lip readers who skipped Scharmon's trope-ridden transitions to get at the "good parts." His stupefying pretense to knowledge-through-suffering excited the blood lust of reviewers everywhere, winning him free and wide publicity. Something for everyone, right?

Alas, right! *I Am That I Am,* the first installment of what would be a serial revelation of one man's serial lapses, went to market and came home a winner. The book certified that the dimly lit promise of Scharmon's youth—oh, about 15 watts' worth—was never to be fulfilled. The critics howled, of course. Judgment was in arrears, but it hadn't yet gone bust. To Scharmon's confession of his itch for celebrity and money and power reviewers hooted "Who cares?" But readers bought ("voted for me," as Scharmon liked to say on talk shows) and the author got square with his licensed audience. He bought a couple of Eames chairs, had his nails manicured, and laid on fat; he satisfied a lifelong ambition to populate his bed with three women at once, but he disappointed them all and himself, which disappointment he retailed in the sequel to *I Am That I Am.*

Now he was talking to Baby Hughie, a onetime writer and now a TV "personality" who had declined to interview Scharmon when he took his squalid story to the Coast to air it to the multitudes. They were talking about the resurgence of white, un-Jewish fiction (What help there for a death sentence on the novel?), and the end of the Wine Boom, and The New Androgeny. For Baby Hughie trend-spotting was life's marrow. He was a mediaperson, and to live he sang of things to come. It was his calling to map land he had never seen and to tell us where we had been before we thought to go there. The future for him appeared at production conferences in the guise of "interesting" guests.

I interrupted them: "Baby Hughie, Jaysus, who's your tailor?"

He pretended not to hear me. Maybe he didn't hear me. His special twist was kid stuff, relevance, the hip boutique. He wore pre-faded jeans cinched by a studded belt, cowpoke's boots, a copper bracelet to fake out the bad karma and evil vibes. What remained of his hair he had gathered into a greasy whisk of ponytail. A fruit? Not on your life. Beneath his cute gear he was as hairy as a gorilla, and if there was anything he admired more dearly than the Youthquake, it was to cork someone— any age would do.

He had carried the Card once upon a time, and he and I had been contributing editors for *The Different Drummer.* I was his apprentice then: social realism was his game, and the Workers were his idols, and Revolution—always—was a-comin'. And then, be damned, it really came, wearing beads, dropping acid, tooting the harmonica and dancing the Monkey. Baby Hughie scrambled aboard. The Revolution passed. Baby Hughie didn't notice.

His memory had begun to short out. Not from too much experimental chemistry, as you might guess. Booze was his vice, he was an old dog, no new tricks after office hours. It was said of him that he had never owned a bottle of Jack Daniel's black for more than two hours. He didn't write much anymore; editors had once called him "Paddy" for his trick of overfilling sentences when he was paid by the word.

He had run out of trends to spring on Scharmon. As the hall filled he was assaulted with a confession: "You know what I realized about myself last night?" I groaned; Baby Hughie did not feign engagement. "I've been using my pecker for a sword . . ."

"Beat it into a plowshare," I suggested. "If you prick us, do we not bleed?" I asked.

And Scharmon, receiving as from afar a feeble signal, confused by static and rival broadcasts, telling him he was without an audience, whuffled a little whine: "Well, if you aren't interested . . ."

"We aren't," Baby Hughie said.

The affair was not beginning happily. Workmen had removed from the lectern the corporate coat of arms of the Marlin LePage chain and replaced it with the pen and inkhorn emblem of Writers Inc. Now, muttering, they returned, and it was off with Writers Inc. and on with the Great Seal of the United States, which was indistinguishable in number of eagles and olive branches and sentiment from Mr. LePage's own: the Vice-President had been dropped by helicopter, unannounced, to rain down upon us his benedictions and his homilies. He began ahead of schedule, understandably eager to be done with us, and was cruising through a speech about the gravity of Memorial Day (all-purpose rhetoric, recyclable on other national holidays) and the jolly rewards of a strapping good read while the delegates continued to drift toward their seats. They were confused; the convention's speeches would be subjected to simultaneous translation, but the delegates were unfamiliar with the talking earmuffs, and as they dragged their shopping bags along the crowded aisles they tangled what was already a jungle of wires, crossing circuits and shorting many of them out. Meantime, conspicuous in the wings, crew-cut Secret Service men stood at full ready, their hands inside their jackets, resting on pistol butts. And the Vice-President, happily oblivious to all realities, rattled along.

The delegates, most of whom now sat warm-eared in dead headphones, had found on their seats what is wistfully called a "fact sheet" giving the curricula vitae of we several samurai. These little biographies were enclosed within presentation copies of the inspirational autobiography of Marlin LePage, *Be My Guest,* printed and bound by Selfservice Press. The delegates used this book, or the fact sheet, in the way that confused guests at a Sunday service of some foreign faith use the prayer book and hymnal: they leafed through the pages or rattled the sheet, counterfeiting comprehension and approval.

Suddenly, after the house had filled and settled down, the Vice-President turned solemn on us and invited "each and every good citizen" to rise and address the American flag. His hand covered his heart: "I pledge allegiance to the flag of the United States of America, and to the Republic for which it stands . . ."

Most delegates lumbered to their feet, mumbling the oath. There were dissidents, of course; the British and Northern Irish sang, and not sotto voce, "God Save the Queen." But the Mainland Chinese, accommodating to a fault, pledged away, winning a grin of thanksgiving from Fugelman—first row, center—and a comradely salute from the Veep.

Who then disappeared, as mysteriously as he had materialized, leaving the next move to me. I cleared my throat: "Settled down? Ready to dive into it?" I shambled to the lectern, hoped I was tall enough to pull off a slouchy lope, I reckoned they always tumbled for a cowboy. Whoever "they" were—I could not distinguish them. I patted my pocket: my glasses were there, I was afraid to put them on. I gave them the lantern jaw, the resonant, drawly voice, the sleepy look: quite deadly, I hoped.

"It's customary to begin such proceedings as these with a snarl at the topic. *The Death of the Novel.* I could say the rubric is demonstrably false, or frivolous, or presumptuous. That it is too broad, too narrow. That it is all effect, no cause. That *Who Killed Cock Novel* would be more provocative. Well, it's my title and my topic, and I like them. Just as these fellows, one an entertainer and the other a tattler, are putatively my creatures, for the moment." (Fugelman, sitting with his stubby legs crossed, shot me a look, a warning shot across my bow. This I saw with perfect acuity.) "Some have said that time, dumb time, has killed fiction." (A Luceman, covering for the Jackie-O page, scowled. But he didn't leave in protest. Question: Why did I not leave in protest?) "Not the magazine, the shortage. Of time. Do you understand?" (They did not understand. Did I?) "Though he is the youngest of your panelists" (looking at Baby Hughie), "Scharmon has committed two successful acts of . . . literature, of a kind. He has made a killing. By making available to anyone with the price of a book the most unutterable details of his private life."

I paused frequently during this devious presentation. My delivery was a politician's, a preacher's, a stand-up comic's. I'd leave silent spaces to be filled with huzzahs (there were none) or laughter (it was not friendly) or to imply irony. I used these silences to plan, to amend silently what I had just said aloud, to complete, for the sake of some private decency, a metaphor which my spoken words had only begun. During these pauses, to give evidence that my synapses were busy, I'd cock an eyebrow, moan a mute moan of disgust, perhaps even wink.

"Scharmon knows his subject, and wants you to know it also. The truth is at once his master and his servant. Though he once itched like all of us to write fiction, such an enterprise would now, I guess, be for him a waste of time and surely of money. It has been said of your first speaker that he has hit the dollar sign on his IBM so hard and so often that it is now quite worn-out, and rings up a broken upper-case *S*. They say he could sell his literary correspondence to *Business Week*. The same could be said of James Joyce, of course, so there you are, nowhere. They say . . . but enough of what *they* say, not that what they say could possibly damage him more than what he has said about himself. I merely fear that whatever I might tell you about this speakthrift will bring down his lawyers, waving fistfuls of torts, charging me with infringement of copyright. So, let Scharmon talk!

"Who reads novels? I want every man here, every woman, every person who has read a full-length work of fiction to its completion within the past couple of weeks to raise his or her right hand."

My God! They were raising their hands! Fugelman was beaming, he loved it, authentic hokum.

"Most of you are lying," Scharmon said. "Thanks for the generous send-off, Jupe." (Very light irony there, or none: this was thick skin.) "I used to be bullied by schoolmarms. 'Never begin a letter with *I*' they'd lisp, and 'Never say *I* in an essay.' They told me *I* was the dirtiest character in the lexicon." (I thought of my eyes, and rubbed them, and felt the lights continue to screw down on me.) "Well, screw them! Screw schoolmarms!" (I wondered what the translation into Nepalese would sound like.) "I, I, *I!* I am I, and here's my story, the only story I know, from the beginning."

The delegates were restless. A fugitive disturbance kicked my conscience: suppose out there among the hundreds were a Beckett, a Borges in the making, a Grass, a Solzhenitsyn, may God deliver him! Suppose there were someone of talent, or even of taste, among the hundreds. Unlikely, of course, but even so, I speedread their faces in case I owed apologies to others besides myself. The television lights blinked off when Scharmon began his long unwinding—who could blame them? —so I could see the audience.

What a thing to be able to see! What a mob of greenhorns! *Hey, Warsaw! Yeah, you with the mouth, shut it, the moths are escaping. . . .* So I thought I was Lenny Bruce. Not even Bruce. Don Prickles, Jupe Rickles, with a First in Greats from Balliol. What a timepiece I was: accurate to a degree when I ran, dangerously false when irregularities of climate or usage upset my delicate movement. What a silly, self-indulgent thing to think! People shouldn't have minded me, shouldn't let me trouble them. I was just confused, just couldn't comprehend why some multiplication tables were duller than others and why, unlike everyone else, I could not endure the fumes of chestnuts roasting on an open fire. But there was no real contest between me and "them" because there was a fix in. I wasn't fighting bad times, not really. I was going through a dumb show, going a couple of rounds with a couple of pushovers. The purse wasn't even that good. I knew it was no noble way to pass time, disapproving, *secretly* disapproving, of the libels some tinhorn hawker, some twopenny mouthpiece like Scharmon, committed against the fiction I had never made. I listened, or pretended to listen, and worked to erase whatever malice was visible on my face, and heard this, or something like it:

". . . so I finally realized that the only kind of narrative worth writing, or reading, was first-person narrative. Why? Because the writer who distances himself from his material is a coward, unworthy of a real man's respect or patronage. No writer worth his salt should hide behind a make-believe spokesperson, or try to pretend that he's a god. That isn't fiction, it's bullshit!"

Evidently *bullshit,* the word, gave offense, and puzzled the translators. A delegate raised his hand, as he had raised it to report his reading habits. Another rose, and faced the flag. A French poet called for a motion of censure, and there were cries from the British of "Bad taste, bad taste!" Scharmon, proof against all men's decent opinions, went forward:

"So I looked around for an *I* who could represent me to the world, and I made up stories for him to tell. But he wasn't as interesting to me as the real me was. How could he have been as interesting to you, my dear readers? And the stories I invented for him were never as extraordinary as the things that really happened to me. Events too bizarre for fiction, that would overload its narrow channels, were the merest banalities of my days. I—Scharmon—experienced the assassination of a President and his brother. Now, it wasn't so much the events themselves that I cared about—what *happened,* as it were— but how they related to *me.* And so I realized that fiction was an evasion of my responsibilities as a man and, yes, as an artist. Fiction is a mug's game, a waste of time to write and of money to buy. Who killed the novel? Honest men like me: I did. I am I at last because I have accompanied myself through the dangerous territories, and have come out the other side holding my own hand. Ambitious? Of course. Successful? I won't deny it. To deny my success would be to deny truth. To deny truth is to deny art. To deny art is to deny myself. To deny myself is to deny my success. See? If you've read my books—and if you haven't you will, believe me—you'll catch my drift. Thank you, thank you, dear hearts, dear good people . . ."

And Scharmon, blowing kisses at the still, dead eye of the television camera, returned to our table and whispered to me, "How'd I do? Knock 'em dead? Bomb? Don't shit me, be honest . . ."

"Buzz-buzz Scharmon, but—what is your word?—*honest* buzz-buzz." And I walked to the lectern, itching to hang a mouse on the shit-heel's eye, and saw Fugelman shaking his head, more in anger than in sadness. What was his beef? Scharmon was his boy.

I looked at Baby Hughie, grinned, looked away. "As aged as my friend is, he's as fit as an electric fiddle. A muscle man who has built bridges to the future, a prophet of fads in consciousness and expression. His *Crawdaddy* piece, declaring that intellection is outmoded, and putting on sandwich boards for ecstasy, is notorious. At the first echo of the first girlish wail that trailed John, Paul, George and Ringo offstage your next speaker shed the poor rags of his youthful purpose and bedecked himself in motley. Don't laugh! Not that you seem capable of laughter. This man has his uses. He is a middleman, beaming the kiddies across kiddiewaves to our television sets, to *your* television sets rather. Raise your hands, everyone who watches this man on television. High now, I can't see you. Come on, you raised your hands for Scharmon, be nice to old Jupe. Aren't you interested in the young? Don't leave, children! I do not wish to offend! I thought I was among grownups or I would have tempered my words. It has been a long day for us all, these past forty minutes. Let me bring this to a close, lest I drive more of you away, and give you the aging hipster himself . . . Hugh."

Fugelman, like a vice-squad dick watching his first skin movie, was scribbling notes to himself, collecting evidence to bring before the executive committee of Writers Inc., to bring before the National Institute of Arts and Letters, to bring to the Op-ed page of the *Times*. He had been screwed. He was beyond fear. Not only had I foisted on him a couple of dead-beats, one of them hadn't showed up and I was dumping on the other! I could see it in his eyes: he wouldn't pay. Why shouldn't he stiff the musicians, and have their union cards pulled? They'd ruined his party. What a terrible screwing he had suffered! And what now, a *hippie?* Even that:

"Well, can you dig it? I feel like a lion about to be thrown to the Christians. Jupe knows all the tricks, all the holds, we go way back. Hell, I got his first piece published. I mean by that that I got his first essay published, not that I got an essay by his chick published. Twenty years ago. Jupe was ahead of us all in those days. Lord, he loved to read books, everybody's books. Novels, of course. He'd strip them down, find the burned valve or collapsed piston, rebuild, give an avuncular scolding to the careless idiot who had built imperfectly, send him forth to make better work next time. Time passed, you know? He stayed here, I went West, left this old town and its old folks. Well, old buddy, old Jupe, let me tell you: a prairie fire has swept this land, will sweep it again, and out where I live we're trying to light it, and it's going to burn away all the old farts like you—and *you,* booing me—gonna burn you away in the blue stink of your old gas. Divine con-sum-mation, man. The Stones are rolling, have already rolled over your grammars, gonna break the spines of your books, gonna kill Massa Novel daid. The kids—"

(The *kids.* Oh my battered cortex: what the keeds are doing, what the keeds want. The Technicolor scene, mind-fucking, fanship. They could have their con if they'd just let my syntax be. Besides, they'd soon be as old as Baby Hughie. Keeds were already buying Winnebagos and looking ahead to their grand-keeds. Pat Boone had made the cover of *Rolling Stone*. Did no thing endure? I suspected that imaginative literature could endure. There: my confession. Sealed.)

"—today are in a hurry. What was the novel for? Once upon a time it brought the news, laid out social arrangements for a new middle class, displayed fashions. Things changed slowly then. Now someone begins a novel that imitates the way people talked the year before, when he began making notes for the silly goddamned thing. A year later, if he's quick, he finishes the book. A year after that it's published. The world it describes is three years old, two and a half years dead. Who needs it? If the story can't be told by the end of this week, it isn't worth telling. Old guys don't like to believe this, they like to believe in what they call standards, right? What's good, what's bad, what will hang in there, what will not. Jupe looks down on us mass-cult boys, look at his face, it spells *v-u-l-g-a-r*. Don't deny it . . ."

"Whatever you say, Hugh, I wouldn't dispute you . . ."

"What's the difference anymore. Fact is, Jupe, there aren't any rules left to break; all the regulations, what you call standards, have gone bye-bye. Who cares, beyond a mob of necktie-choked professors who are paid to pretend to care? Yeah, I'm pointing at him. Now we—"

(Did that accusing finger rest on me? It did. *Careful with those "we's," lad, easy does it, a little long in the tooth now for "we's" with crooners and miniswingers.* He should have been wise and sad, like the best of us. It was instructive to have seen it rise and fall, to have felt the wave lift us, crest, and let us down. *Too late to be a beachboy, old man, surf's down now.*)

"—get our news from our music, and our men of letters are

men of song. Singers, as poets once were, in bygone times. Tom
Waits is a great poet, though not as great as Dylan. Not *your*
Dylan, Jupe, I'm wailing about Mr. Chops, Bob."

(*My* Dylan? Baby Hughie got me. You had to keep an eye
on Baby Hughie, the old bastard could still win a throw or two.
One Dylan was as bad as the next in my Palgrave's.)

"Now dig me, I'm gonna leave you with a song."

(!!!!!!!)

"Sail the sea of madness,
Poot you readin' down.
Do some groovy badness,
Poot that dead thing *down!*
Squeeze some juice,
Slip you noose,
Don't read, heed
The ragman,
Tatterin'
DEATH TO WHOLES!"

And Baby Hughie was gone, right offstage, not waiting for
the applause he never would have heard, because there was
none. I noticed a delegate playing pocket pool with one hand,
stifling a yawn with the other. A couple of others were reading
the news, rattling the pages to get at the early race results.
Fugelman's eyes were puffy and red. I scooped together a deck
of index cards and looked over the house, and it was bad.
Fugelman was a hanging judge; there was a lynch mob out
there, and I'd be lucky to reach home wearing my hide. The
delegates who had stayed the distance broke into two camps:
Central Europeans and Exotic Rowdies. The first bunch wore
last-a-lifetime brogans and sturdy, sensible suits of high-sheen
gabardine, dyed dark to hide stains and cut full to accommo-
date a twenty percent weight increase, just in case. They

bought their pipe tobacco wholesale, could fix the hotel plumbing when it acted up, and believed only in preventive maintenance on the family sedan. They had been taking notes during our vaudeville so they could report to the Kultchur Klubs back home What Was Happening. They were the kind who transcribed their lecturer's "good morning" in shorthand at the beginning of every class, and his "thank you," underscored twice, at the end.

The rowdies came in many colors, and were dressed in djellabahs and caftans and saris and fezzes, tribal robes and wooden clogs and rubber-tire sandals. Some were tattooed; one of them, front and center, a man whose face bespoke both wit and learning, wore a bone through his nose.

I looked over the racial patchwork of Slavs and Sikhs, of Cubans wearing bandoleers and muddy field boots, of Gabonese verse dramatists and Tanzanian new-wavers, and then . . . I prolonged my silence. Fugelman, to put me at ease, drew his finger across his throat in a savage cutting swipe. I stared down at my index cards, then shuffled them as a shark might, then bent them back with a dexterous bridge, then did my waterfall. "Want to see some card tricks?" I had begun my five-hundred-dollar lecture.

Fugelman broke. He was on his feet, windmilling his arms. "You wise-ass bastid. You're washed up in this racket. Who needs you?" And he steamed up the aisle to the lobby, his feet churning like a bicycle racer's, to begin his telephone calls.

I hoped his outburst might draw me some sympathy. It did not. I stared at an index card. It was scratched upon by my scribble, but squint as I might, I could not decode it. Now a headache blurred my vision. I could see far but not near. Words close up burned my eyes; names fell on my head, or tumbled like dirty laundry inside it. Notions proliferated and died, their corpses mingled and bloated till I thought my brain cage would crack trying to contain them. Another couple of writers left, hustling ass to get to Korvettes before it shut for the weekend. I drew from my pack, picked a card, any card:

"Surely it was Robert Craft who said that Huxley said that Eliot's criticism is like a 'great operation that is never performed: powerful lights are brought into focus, anaesthetists and assistants are posted, the instruments are prepared. Finally, the surgeon arrives and opens his bag—but closes it again and goes off.' It is fitting, is it not, since we are occupied, this band of brothers, these happy kinsmen still imprisoned here together . . . I'm afraid I've lost the trail through that sentence. How did I begin? Ah, yes! Diseased novel, reluctant surgeon-critic, dead novel. Well, in fact I jotted down Huxley's judgment not because of its application to Eliot, or to his criticism, but because it applies to me. As, in fact, a would-be, in fact, fictioneer."

Others made for the exits, and I turned a carny routine against them:

"Don't leave, boys, the taverns are dead this time of day, full of round-the-clock topers, the hookers are still asleep, stick around, hear me out, LISTEN TO ME GODDAMMIT! . . . Listen, please. I know a funny story. Once upon a time there was a novelist. I don't like him now, but I did then, when he was down on his luck. He taught Principles of Composition at Herkimer Jerkimer High on Staten Island, worked nights on his second novel, the first having disappeared without trace a few minutes after it was published one Sunday morning at four o'clock. Many mornings this poor scribbler would sleep through his alarm, miss the ferry, and show up late for this first class. So the principal bearded my old friend and laid it out:

'Come late once more, Mr. Fancywords, and you're canned,
you can work with your hands.' Now, this was a *malediction!*
So the poor bastard—he was a poor bastard *then*—kept writing, but he forced himself awake in proper time every morning
for a week. He bought another alarm clock. He even took in
a cat—he hated cats—that jumped on his bed every sunup and
licked him awake, wanting something. But it happened again:
he overslept because he trusted the cat, so the cat overslept. He
sweated out a subway ride to the Battery, got to the dock a few
minutes past eight, saw his boat five, six feet from the pier. It
was December. He saw the white water churning out from the
screws, he saw garbage in the water, he had less than a second
to decide. Should he gamble on the jump? Maybe miss, and
sink? Or should he let them fire him, and die slowly, from want
of food? 'What the fuck!' he shouted, top of his voice. He
boiled down the pier, leapt, just made it, fell face forward on
the icy deck, tore the knees out of his pants, heard them all
laughing: the boat was coming in . . . There's a moral hidden
there . . . I loaned five hundred dollars to this guy. He wanted
the dough to have his teeth capped so he'd enjoy a more
winning smile. Thought it would help that second novel to
have a comely, go-to-hell face smiling off the back jacket. It
must have. When the book was published four months later,
and he had sold club and paper and movie rights, I tried to get
my half a yard back, but he wouldn't pay me. I squeezed him
hard, and finally he gave me the first draft of his first novel, a
holograph script, and he signed it, and told me if I hung on
to it it would be worth a lot more than five hundred bucks. I
burned it. It would be worth a lot more than five hundred
bucks.''

A man was standing in the aisle, pointing his cane at me. I
saw it all at once: the delegate from fancy's suicide squad, come

to cut me down. *All right, men, he's got the goods on us, the obituary must be stopped and hang the cost. The critic is dead, long live the novel! Wimpy, you've drawn the short straw. Use the cane gun. Don't fail us, and don't expect to return alive. Your name will endure, for a while, in the* International Authors and Writers Who's Who: 1977. *Cut him down; he deserves no better . . .* Where were the Secret Service gunslingers now that I needed them? The man was screaming at me, and then I recognized his trench coat. He was an American, a fixture at such affairs as this, the Conscience of the New York Intellectual Community.

"In God's name, when will you cease the bombing!"

"They say the war is over, sir."

"In God's name, when will the lying cease!"

"Don't point your petition at me, you fool. I'm not the Vice-President, he left hours ago."

"When will Americans take responsibility for the crimes done in their names!"

There was sustained applause, the first of the day, from the few hangers-on; the rabble-rouser acknowledged it with a shy grin, and left. Behind me the dais was empty: Scharmon had escaped. There were maybe half a dozen people in the audience. Two were definitely asleep, two more were probables. A woman in the balcony sat on a man's lap. Her back was to me. They did not sit still. And there was another. I saw him dimly. He sat at the back of the orchestra, wearing army fatigues, soaking up every word, getting it all down in his black account book. His face was masked by the shadow thrown by the balcony, but I thought I recognized him. He was my own shadow, masking me. The girl in the balcony was still; her associate made motions as though to leave. They left, separately. The sleepers slept. I turned to my phantom amanuensis:

"You, hanging back there where I can't make you out. It seems we're alone, alone among the waking in any case. Come closer, why don't you, so I can steal a proper look at you, and finish up without shouting."

He made no move toward me.

"What's your name, then? You have a solemn look, strong chin, busy fingers. What do they call you? I know you, you know? It's true, my memory's off, but I'll recollect your name, give me a moment."

Did he grin? As though he knew the treacherous habits of my memory? Too much reviewing had burned it out. I'd blitz up some subject like the North African novel and no sooner write it out of my wits than I'd be drumming up intelligence for "The History of Censorship" or "The Trouble with Dickens." My mind had become a child's magic slate, written upon, erased, written upon anew, every blank space covered with names, theories, disputes, the plastic sheet pulled from the magic surface, amazement! The slate was clean! Dope out the stuff, write it, forget it. Nothing persisted for me. All ripened fast, and fell before its season. I would never recall his name, his dates, his place, his achievement. His anonymity, as he seemed to know, was secure.

"I'll continue, then. Wasn't it Pound who remarked . . . who stated . . . who claimed . . . hang on, I'll find it, I wouldn't have lost it, I'm sure, ah, here we are, Pound: 'Everything that I touch, I spoil. I have blundered always.' What do you think of that, sir?"

He was sitting on his hands, shaking his head, displaying pity not for Pound but for me. His mouth was pursed, as though he might be saying *tsk, tsk, tsk.*

"Identify yourself, God damn you! What are you? A stanzifier? Make-believer? You're a make-believer, I knew it. Long-haul trucker or short-stroker? A reader, then? What are your credentials? Your intentions? By what right do you judge me? Why?"

But I was sweating a shadow, and four sleeping writers with shopping bags in their laps.

I walked home from the LePage. By the time I got there Kate already knew about my fiasco: "Jupe, dear Jupe, I'm so sorry . . ."

"Who told you?"

"Nick stopped by, to borrow a book."

"Who told him?"

"Someone, I don't know. And Fugelman called, at least I think it was Fugelman. He ranted about show biz, and real troupers who knew how to play to a house. He said he'd pay you back someday soon, wait and see, but it sounded more like a threat than a promise of a check."

I twisted a smile out of myself. "Are you worried?"

"I guess so, a bit, why shouldn't I be?"

Not to fear, I told her. Mind was running fast, that was all. Like clear water—what had Nick told me? Like clear water over sharp stones, tumbling down the mountain. There were sometimes cataclysms. Streambed troubled . . . freshet changing course . . . boulders dislodged. Generally such adjustments transpired in private corners of the forest, where no one heard or noticed. The confusion would cease, the geography would be discovered one day to have altered, all would be still again.

"But your metaphorical stream got quite a few people's feet wet, and not in a corner of the forest but at a convention of people who do what you do—I think they're called *peers.*"

I yielded to her there, conceded the distinction to be made.

"I won't ask you why you staged such a horror show, but I will ask whether you have your reasons, whatever they are. Do you know what you're doing?"

"Burning bridges?"

"That is a question, I had hoped for an answer."

"Not to worry, Kate. Okay?" Then I told her I wanted to go to the reception that night for Writers Inc. To show my face, mount up after my fall.

"Of course. I'll get a baby-sitter."

I found Robin seated at my desk, constructing backwards B's and upside-down F's, writing them on the faces of my index cards.

"How did it go today, chum?"

"Well, I can't read again today, and I can't write too. I fell downstairs this morning. Someone stole my bicycle."

"Much like my own experience. Pretty poor excuse for a day, right?"

"Well, it's better than nothing." He had a point.

"Let me tell you a story."

"Sure. Which book?"

"No book," I said. "I'm sick of books. I'll make one up, sort of."

"I'd like that," my son said.

So I sat on the big leather couch, and it felt solid and cool against my back. The late-afternoon sun was hot, and it angled through the bars behind my dirty basement window and fell on Robin's fair hair spread across my lap. It would have fit the occasion to invent sweet tales of Provident Squirrel and Sly Fox, but such fiction was beyond my reach. The best I could offer was a parable built upon a few facts.

"Once upon a time there was an Oxford student, an American, who liked to eat dinner at an Indian curry parlor. The place was cheap, and they served other kinds of food, too, mostly English, and if you took pains with what you ordered, the food tasted okay, good, pretty good. One night the student ordered curried chicken, and it tasted very, very good to him. Perhaps it was because he was disposed to be pleased—he had just received a letter from a beautiful princess who had agreed to marry him . . ."

"Mommy?"

"Don't interrupt. Perhaps the chicken curry tasted wonderful for reasons other than the way it really tasted, but for whatever reason, it gave pleasure. So the student went back, night after night, and asked always for the same thing. But he never got it. A Chinese waitress worked in the Indian restaurant. She was cheerful, in fact her good will was relentless. She wrote down every word of my order in her odd little characters, odder even than your own letters and numbers. I . . ."

"I already guessed you were the hero."

I squeezed his dry hand. "I'd look over her shoulder and imagine I saw the ideogram of steaming curried chicken, with chutney, and my anticipation was extreme. But the stuff never came. The Chinese waitress would deliver boiled mutton, or a fried egg on fried bread, never curried chicken. And when I'd object, she'd smile her kind smile, and cheerfully admit her error, and promise me that I'd enjoy her substitution better than my order. And because I was green then, and cordial, and shy . . ."

"Like me?"

"Not so green as that, and not so cordial. And because she was so forceful—*Don't worry*, she'd say, *alla same good, chicken and pig and sheep, alla same nice guy, taste good*—I'd eat what was put before me, and never complain. And it tasted awful! Lord, Robin, I can still taste it. Then I grew up. And began to complain. People paid me to recognize the taste of things, and complain if they tasted awful."

"I wouldn't eat things that don't taste good, even for money."

"Someone has to."

"Why?"

"Never mind. I was good at it, ask your mother, I really was. People tried to talk me out of things, like the Chinese waitress, and like the Chinese waitress, people tried to talk me into things, but I held the line. People still try to bend the line; they say things that aren't true, and I don't know why."

"Who are they?"

"Who?"

"The people you call *they*. Who does bad things to you?"

"Well, I don't know, I guess there are so many of them, it's hard to say exactly. I don't know, they're everywhere you look . . ."

"Am I, Daddy?"

"Are you what?"

"Am I *they?*"

"Of course not. You don't know how to write, don't even know how to read."

"But I'm going to learn how to read."

"Of course. Of course you are."

The baby-sitter asked me whether I understood Spanish, and because she was staring Ortega y Gassett square in his title page I confessed that, yes, I could get by in her primary language. So even before we knew each other's names she asked me to translate her life story into English, she spoke more poetically in Spanish, we'd share royalties, sixty-forty, the big piece to her, it was her life, after all, and what a life! The woman had a tangled, wild look, and I dared not offend her moments before surrendering my son to her care, so I said it was an inviting proposition but that there were certain calls on my time. She complained that when Oscar Lewis had passed through her neighborhood with his tape recorder he had not even asked to hear an outline of her life story. I confessed that I had heard similar charges brought against Professor Lewis by others living in New York. I promised her that as soon as my desk was clear, I'd be on her case. She gathered Robin to her bosom, he winked at me, I winked at him, Kate and I left.

We walked from Gramercy Park toward the LePage on Central Park South. We passed the Union League Club on lower Park Avenue and I caught an old geezer staring out the window at Kate, his face a mask of envy. Little wonder: she was pleasing to the eye. She had a straight-ahead gait, leaning forward, eager to get on, sexy. She had been talking to me, but my mind was elsewhere.

"What was that? I'm sorry."

"I said that old gentleman smiled at me. He looks like Baby Hughie, what do you think?"

I offered my arm, and she took it. We worked north without talking till Grand Central blocked our way, then we dodged through side streets, and the crowds thickened and jostled us, and we had to make our way single-file, like soldiers on patrol, till we reached Fifth Avenue. Like a blind man I let Kate lead, but once on Fifth the people kept more decent distance one from another, and we came abreast again. I was busy thinking: I had insulted friends and enemies alike, without fear or favor. I had given way to bizarre impulses without resisting them, like the legendary guy who rides the New York subways weeping to provide grist for Pete Hamill's mill, and Jimmy Breslin's. The guy who can't stand any more rudeness, or indifference, or filth, or noise, or heat, or cold. The guy forever stuffing dimes in the gum machine, forever having no gum tumble down the chute. The guy who never wises up about the gum machines because he can't believe they'll keep stiffing him. The guy who finally wises up, beats the shit out of the gum machine, gets busted, weeps, and shows up next day in the *Post* or *Daily News,* next week in the *Voice.*

The insults paid my own psyche were different, of course, but no less violent. Or so it seemed to me. Within the past ten days I had been telephoned awake by a radio interviewer: "What do you think about crime? Plan to change your locks? How about the sexual revolution? For or against? Is there one? If there isn't, what is the Supreme Court cracking down on? Do you believe in the literary situation? Are you mad at Truman Capote? You don't know him? That's funny, he said he didn't know you, either. What did you think of his masked ball? What *do* you believe in?"

We were crossing Fifth at Central Park South against the light, arm in arm. I hadn't noticed the light change; horns blew at us, drivers shrieked abuse, and we were trapped midstream. I tried to speak to Kate, but she couldn't hear me above the racket till the light had changed again and we had reached the far shore.

We stood for a moment in the dying light, looking up the length of Central Park, past the lights of Harlem, far north. In fact we were only pretending to lift our sight such a far distance: I knew that Kate's eyes, like mine, were narrowed, and focused near. We seldom heard each other's silences, but that day I heard mine, and when I broke it I could scarcely recognize the run and pitch of my voice.

"The sap's flowing. It's time to go north. Maybe Monday."

"But we aren't ready, Jupe. Robin's school . . . I haven't done anything about having the house opened . . ."

"I want to get away. I think I'd better go alone."

She actually stamped her foot; I heard the angry click, steel on concrete. People stared at us, tempestuous lovers we must have seemed, nothing odd in that part of town, except perhaps we were a bit old for our parts. I was patient. Her color was up: "When are we to come?"

"Maybe it's not a good idea this summer. The book . . ."

"Screw the book. We'll leave you in peace while you write, we've always left you in peace, haven't we? What's so special about this book?"

"I might try something different, more important, something . . . different."

"Don't give me that crap, Jupe, we're beyond kid stuff by now, aren't we? Let us come with you. I'll take Robin out of school early, what difference can a few weeks make?"

"I need to leave right away. Would you rather have me go

to Yaddo? The MacDowell Colony? I don't want to be plain about it, to you of all people. You always understood, so understand: I want to be alone, have to be alone for a while."

"Okay, bub, you're alone."

And she turned away. A less subtle lover would have crossed into the treacherous night-noises of the park, leaving me to fear for her sanctity and to agonize over my cruelty. That was not her way. She let me walk her to the taxi rank in front of the Plaza, and give her some money. Then, no tears in evidence, she gave our home address and was driven off. No incomplete sentences, sobs, insults. I watched the taxi till it disappeared. She never looked back. I thought she would.

I walked toward the LePage, and when I looked behind me, he was there, like the ghost from some quotidian nightmare. He was shaking his head again, sadly again, as though he had received bad news about me. I resolved to erase him, the way a novelist would erase a character for whom he had no further use. I shot the shadow a finger, held the middle finger of my writing hand erect from my fist and shook it at him. He didn't disappear. Passers-by stared at my vulgar gesture; they looked like the same passers-by who had moments before stared at Kate and me; everyone looked alike, everywhere. I held my fist aloft like a standard while I pressed forward to the gathering of the tribes.

The auditorium had been rigged out to serve as a reception hall. I made my entrance from backstage and stood for a moment where I had stood a few hours earlier at the lectern, now gone and, I hoped, forgotten. It was time for the glasses, and I fished them from my pocket, and hooked them over my ears. They were grotesque, Coke-bottle lenses in a heavy horn frame. Their effect was shocking, snapping what had been mercifully dim into bright focus. I saw as I had seen when I was young, but how awfully the world had changed.

The huge room was windowless, but fake velvet, with drum majorette's gold tassels weeping from its tails, had been draped to hide the windows that weren't. The corporate motto of LePage Enterprises was upon these hangings, telling in Latin of laundromats, houseboats, bowling alleys, oil shale, soda pop and hotels. LePage Himself was at the hall's opposite end from me, hanging gilt-framed, nine feet by four, wearing riding breeches, holding a whip, scowling, in the company of a white horse and a borzoi.

His costume was more commonplace than most I saw below me as I looked down and through the smoke at the kind of bedlam experienced during a fire panic. There were fewer glasses than people, and everyone wanted two drinks. It looked like the contest parade of a fancy-dress masquerade: *Come as kitsch,* the invitation would have insisted. Feather boas, chain mail, patent-leather hip boots with killer heels for the ladies; ruffled shirts, wooden crosses, nut-hugger trousers for the gents. I thought of the animals at circuses, so pathetically got up to look like people, the bears and monkeys in bib overalls, the seals in skirts, slapping their flippers in a monstrous parody of good times.

I searched for a familiar face down there in the cockpit, and realized that in some confused way all the faces were familiar. Oh, most of the names were lost to me, or had never been known, but I knew the faces. Middle-rung editors, promoters, out-of-town reviewers, bookshop managers, cultural buccaneers like me . . . The air was sour, polluted by the complaints of ambitious people suffering from ulcers and disappointed appetites. They were spoiled children, bright kids, most of them, whiz-bangs at twelfth-grade English, people who would tell you an hour after you met them that they had scored perfect marks on their College Board verbals, and many of them had. Most of them had announced themselves as Writers before their second college year: writing seemed like a good idea, clean work for a bright, spoiled kid. To go into business for yourself, keep easy hours, make quick killings with the movie folk, score with literate groupies—what could be nicer, more suitable? It wasn't just yachts and pussy, either, there was other stuff: the anthologies, the Nobel, the *à fond* article by Kazin or Kenner. And to have your merest commonplaces reported next morning in the *Times,* here indeed was very heaven.

On what evidence did they base their claims for such a sweet, bookish life to come? Intuition, mostly, and the invincible certitude that what bright, spoiled kids want, bright, spoiled kids had better damned well be given. Hard evidence, too: Creative Writing A and Creative Writing B. I had taught both; I had seen the future, and there it was, on the ballroom floor of the LePage, stampeding for booze. Ex-students who *knew* they were good, because their fellow students had told them so. Log-rollers who had casually read one another's stories every week and criticized them as though they were consequential works: *I like it, it's interesting, there are some interesting things in it, it didn't bore me, I wonder if that's how you spell "tradgic," otherwise it's perfect, pretty interesting.*

And now? Later? Middle-rung editors, promoters, out-of-town reviewers, bookshop managers, would-be novelists, cultural buccaneers like me . . . I had thought I was different, I had thought I had damped my literary delusions. I hadn't thought of myself as a Writer, not in *their* way, not in the way of those hungry, spoiled, bitter mummers and mountebanks, tarted up in their modish caps and bells, mixing their metaphors, wondering what had gone wrong, wondering who was screwing them, why they were always locked out of the interesting wing of the house, the wing they heard all the rumors about.

Surely I was not like them? To look at me was to see the difference: I wore plain gray worsted. Besides, most of them had never truly tried to write anything, had quit before they began. A few did persist in the inexplicable persuasion that they were poets—God knows what else, *novelists*—and these made their wives and employers forever miserable, bitching that their wives and employers had sold them out, when truth was there had never been anything to buy.

Was it any wonder, then, knowing them as I did, having lived in the certainty that I was unlike them, feeling their presumptions begin to infect me, wanting despite myself to ring the chimes with a novel (and about *what*, I might well have asked), is it any wonder that I was not myself? And to whom, if not to Jupe, could I have turned to inquire after the legitimate character of that character? Surely not to *them*, pitlings and pismires?

I came down to their level, and went among them. The foreign guests, in whose honor the reception had been arranged, were bunched together like wallflowers, comparing exchange rates and muggings. An editor bore down on me from across the room. He was the kind of editor who hung out at places like literary receptions, buying properties he would never read. I couldn't recall his name or his affiliation; he was a mover, forever being fired for buying losers or quitting to trade up with his winners.

"Jupe, you ole dawg, where you been hidin', boy?"

Yep, he said "Dawg." Southern dialects had been much in vogue a few years before: Mailer had been using a Georgia sheriff's muddy drawl for his newsmaking homilies, and Grand Ole Opry stars had priority on everyone's guest list. Another fashion in retreat, redneck chic, had just overtaken the editor; yes, of course, it would have to be "dawg."

"I've been around," I told him. "Reading, writing, my number's in the book."

I said this stiffly, imagining myself in the library of London's Athenaeum, dismissing the club nuisance. He gripped my upper arm. An innocent onlooker would think we were preparing to trade punches, but he was trying to be friendly, he was into what they called "tactile communication," what I called "touch," it had been all the cry the year before.

"Jupe, be honest, tell me true. Are you satisfied with your publisher? Level with me."

"Okay. I'm not all that happy, just now I'm most unhappy. But I don't think it would be fair to blame my publisher, you know? Do you agree? Level with me."

He squeezed my wrist. "I understand *perfectly*. Jesus, you're discreet, I love it." He winked at me. "Listen, Jupe"—he was so proud to have remembered my name—"listen. Lunch, late next week, I'll cancel someone out, what the hell. I'd love"— vicious squeeze—"*love* to publish a book by you. Jesus! You're the best we've got. I'm looking for something, you know, big, maybe we can do a deal."

"I'm your man," I lied. "I've got something big," I lied.

"Phone me tomorrow."

"Tomorrow's Sunday."

"Phone me Monday, we'll take a meeting beginning of the week."

"No need to wait," I told him. "I've got the manuscript with me, in the coatroom. Let's get it. You can read it in the lobby, I'll tell you what I want for it, we can work up a contract and both go to bed happy."

"*Now? Here?* You must be kidding. I've heard you've pulled some weird stunts lately, but this is over the limit. You want me to *read* a *book?* Tonight? You've finished a book without showing an outline, without going for an advance?" Cunning peeped through his eyes, his nose flared, he smelled trouble. "What is it, something hot? Controversial? Your publisher turn it down? Why? Legal problems?"

"Absolutely not. It's a big one, needs a big editor, a man who can look beyond the page to the bank vaults yonder. You'll love it." I squeezed his thigh. "It's *you,* by God! I see it on The List, a translation into Arabic, Stanley Kubrick—"

"Look, Jesus, I'd love to see the thing, maybe in a couple of days . . ."

"Nope. Tonight. Now. Or never. It's short, five hundred pages, double-spaced elite. I'll translate the German bits, you know enough French and Latin for the other foreign stuff. Hell, I'll tell you what, put down your drink and come with me now, I'll read it to you aloud, in the lobby, what do you say?"

"I say I've got a date tonight. Wife's with her sister in the country. And this rawbone hound plans to do a little he-ing and she-ing, can you dig it?"

"I'm sorry we can't do business."

"Jesus, so am I." He had already forgotten my name. "Good luck, I hope you find the publisher you deserve." Spoken like a curse.

"Well, you ole dawg, hang in there, y'hear?"

He shook his head in wonder at the sagacity of my parting words.

"Hey, Jupe, I hear you knocked them dead today, what will you do for a living from now on?"

I waved, it could have been anyone. I cocked my ear elsewhere. The air in the room felt heavy; hysterical noises rose and fell, were driven and borne back. Uncertain radio frequencies tuning in and out on a wind-whipped boozy night, sounds of human thunder and lightning, the sounds people make when they do not mean well by one another, familiar sounds.

I was faced by a thatch-haired gentleman wearing a mask of high seriousness, bookish in the extreme, a very dean of men in his salt-and-pepper tweeds.

"Jupe, is that you? Son of a bitch! How long has it been?"

"Couple of years, five maybe. How have you been keeping?"

"Shit, so-so, not so well. I've been teaching around, doing the upstate normals and the agricultural and mechanicals. I'm eating crow, what the hell. My lecture agent dropped me, said I've run out of charisma, for Christ's sake, what old fogies like us used to call *It*, remember?"

"You look honest, must be worth something?"

"Never mind, I keep ends together, do the odd book review, just like you. You know?"

I winced. From time to time our work had shown up in the same sorry periodicals. A lot of people were claiming my kinship, and it was harder every day to repudiate them.

"Sure," I said. "I know. It's the same the whole world over, a bloody shame."

"Oh, shit, I don't know." He wasn't looking for a handout, or for pity. So what was his game? "Hey, Jupe, it's not like the good old days, remember? The *Fanny Hill* trial, *Tropic of Cancer*?"

"Of course I remember. We did *Last Exit to Brooklyn* together, didn't we?"

"Bet your ass. I won *Last Exit* for the defense, don't you remember? Son of a bitch. They ask me, 'What is your considered opinion of this work, Professor?' Says I, 'This book is physic for the cancerous pomp of its diseased patient, the Western world.' A crusher. I didn't know what I was talking about, how could they? Hey, Jupe, don't you yearn for the old days? I haven't had a decent smut trial since *I Am Curious, Yellow.* Cotton was high before the Warren Court fucked us up, right? Travel bucks, per diem, honorarium, the kick of seeing the old name in print. Shit. Say this for Nixon: he gave us a good Court again, one that's generating some business for old-timers like us. You hanging around here these days, the big apple?"

"Yup."

"Well, why not? Shit. This is where it's at, like the kids say. Hate the little fuckers myself, no offense if you happen to like kids. They've gone too far, in my opinion. Know the trouble with kids?"

I confessed that I did not.

"The trouble with kids is that they're too young. Hey, Jupe, can you steer something my way, some young poontang, something easy, just for old times' sake?"

I told him I could not, wished him good hunting.

"I don't care what everyone else is saying, Jupe, you're okay. You and me, we know the ropes, no shit." He tapped his forehead, winked. "You were a real scout, plenty of sand, slogged through the dirt with the best of us, maybe I should say the worst of us. Shit. We rang up the register for the old First Amendment, served our time, did we not, you old son of a bitch?"

"We did indeed."

"Good luck, Jupe. Don't listen to the others, they're just jealous. Aren't they?"

"Of course."

"Yeah, well . . ."

"Well . . ."

I blew Fugelman a kiss. He pretended he didn't see me, pretended I wasn't there.

Nick was talking to a girl, near the bar. She took my interest. Her smile did it, a gleaming bite of teeth as straight and white as a Main Street picket fence. I maneuvered to the bar and ordered a glass of water.

"Water and what?" the bartender demanded.

"Water plain," I said.

"A wise guy," the barman said.

When I joined Nick and the girl she assumed I had brought the glass for her, and she took it from me and thanked me. She seemed to know me, told me right away that she had read and profited from *Another, Better World.* Why was the first book always the book they liked? Her skin was as pale as glossy paper and her eyes were like punctuation marks.

"What a set of specs, Jupe! They become you."

"Be nice, what are you doing here, slumming?"

"Slumming. The lady is picking my brains," Nick said. "She's eager to learn the trick of having a book published . . ."

"It's not my book," she interrupted. "It's a friend's, and it's very special . . ."

Oh, sure, it was always special, and it was always a friend's. *Doctor, I've got this friend, he's got the vee-dee, I want to help him, maybe there's a pill?* They all thought there was a trick to it. Published writers were like Masons: learn the secret grip, say the password, show a letter of introduction to an executive editor, whoosh, there you were, Hemingway. Why did they think I knew the grip? They did. My dentist had asked me, while I was in the chair and his fingers poked around my mouth, to get his novel published. Said it was cute, about a dentist who loved his patient, his shyness, his scheme of calling her back again and again for fillings she didn't need, his declaration of love just after he'd gassed her, her reciprocal affection, the clincher in the chair, what did I say? I said *Mmmmmmmm!* My tax guy at H&R Block, who held in my file the evidence of a felony, begged me to find a publisher for his exposé of tax dodges, a yarn, he assured me, with "plenty of balls on it."

Nick cocked his eye at her. He had even less affection for amateurs than I had. Our high opinion of ourselves was invincible, despite a lot of evidence coming in against us, against me. The lady was a splendid critter, but her clumsy effort to dip trade secrets out of Nick's pocket was too much for him, a man of high principle and high self-interest, and he began to give her the business.

"Tell your friend, Mrs. . . ."

"Mouse."

"Well, Mrs. Mouse . . ."

"Nick, I believe Mouse is the lady's Christian name."

"Yes, I see. Tell your scribbling friend that my own publishing strategy is simplicity itself."

"Please tell me."

"Of course. I deliver my manuscripts to Jupe here. He reads them. Those he likes get published. Those he doesn't like I throw away."

"Do you always trust his judgment?"

"Of course. He's a critic, isn't he? He's got responsibilities, guards the temple doors, bars them against unruly beggars who would foul the font of traditional logic and sequence. Not that Jupe hates fiction, despite what he says. He just can't get most fiction to behave. Really, beneath his snarls you'll hear a lover coo if your friend will only write according to the rules, to Jupe's rules."

The Mouse smiled. "I think my friend would be pleased to write according to your friend's rules."

"Tell him to get in touch with Jupe, for sure. He knows the ropes, it's as easy as that. If Jupe finds a verb in every sentence that holds a noun, Jupe will find a good editor, the kind who doesn't hang around places like this, and you can consider your friend contracted."

The girl stared at me. "Wow," she said. "Wow! Great glasses! Great!" Then, while she took my measure, looking me up and down, she startled me, and not for the last time. She touched my hand and lifted it to her face. I thought she meant to kiss it, or to read my palm, but she was only looking. "That's good," was her judgment. "Calluses on your fingertips. The marks of an artist, of a real typist."

"Are all typists artists?" I asked her.

"Jesus," said Nick. "Jesus Christ." And he left us, walked past the bar without stopping, climbed to the dais, and disappeared through the door I had used for my entrance.

She told me she had been looking for me. I asked whether we had met before. She said we had not, but that she had heard my performance earlier in the day. I asked for her opinion of it. She said that I had surprised her, that she had always regarded creative writers as "holy men." I managed not to laugh in her gorgeous face.

"Are you in books, as the tradesmen say?"

"I'm unconnected right now," she said. "But I'm devoted to literature."

Her beauty was intimidating. She was the kind of woman who spends Saturday night at home alone because no man would imagine she might be free. Men insult such women, perhaps from fear. She was saved from such a hard fate by a marginal flaw, a kind of killing earnestness.

"Well, my devotee, I'm not unconnected. I have a wife and a son, and I think I would like to take myself home to them."

She seemed not to take account of my determination to leave. "Tell me, why do you hate creative writers?" Her question sounded unfelt, as though she were speaking from the deep well of hypnosis. Her voice seemed as indifferent to the words it launched as a printing press is indifferent to the characters it stamps on blank paper. I glanced at her chest, swollen in a most lifelike and inviting manner against her dress. The dress was a cotton thing, simple and light, not of that place or that epoch. I stared, puzzled, because there was something, despite her beauty, sexless about her.

"I don't hate them," I lied. "At least I don't think I hate them. I thought it would be fun . . . yes, I guess fun is the word I want . . . I thought it would be fun to ask the unaskable: What earthly good are they? But then I forgot to ask."

"Every poem has as much reason for being as the earth and the sun."

I waited for her to continue. The line was not unknown to me, the words were not hers, but that didn't in itself offend me. No one's words seemed any longer to belong to their latest author, everyone stole. Her taste, though, was florid. Her voice flowed on, droning dead noises.

"Do you know Claude Bernard?"

"Is he in books?" I asked, laughing.

She neither smiled nor blinked, but drove straight through my frivolity. "Claude Bernard, 1813–1878, said this: 'If I had to define life in a word, it would be: life is creation.' So you see . . . Well, how would you answer that?"

"It's a nice homily, Mouse, but I'd say that this is a mighty raffish setting, given the hucksters all around, the living lies to his aphorism, for Monsieur Bernard."

So she smiled. Didn't merely exhibit her teeth, as she had exhibited them earlier to Nick and to me, but truly smiled, her first human reflex in my company, and I found it . . . winning. She touched my hand again, and I sensed that a hurricane was making up down south, and that I had better take closer notice of the weather signs before I got blown away. I was no adulterer, betrayal had never been my vice.

"I really dig you," she said.

"You *what* me?" Her declarative sentence was more animated than her previous blowzy sentiments, but the locution lifted my gorge.

"We must seize the day."

Okay, I had had enough. She was out of bounds, and probably off balance. I couldn't deal with her, it was time to head down the road, maybe I could catch Nick in the lobby, bring him home to dinner. I addressed the lady so curiously known to herself as Mouse in my most Edmund Wilsonian periods, lacing my speech with cautions: "Young ladies should not play with strangers, married strangers, old strangers, serious strangers."

So then she reached up, not far, she was tall, and clasped her fingers behind my neck, and dug in, and brought our mouths together. She gave off a peculiar smell, more disinfectant than perfume, a smell of black chemistry. I felt her breasts press against my pens; there was something artificial to her, as to me.

"Did you like that?" she asked, not coyly.

What could I say? I reminded her that we were on display. She was indifferent. I had imagined that the yammering all around us had ceased while the eyes of the world described by *Publishers Weekly* swung on a single stalk to stare at us. But then I took the disloyal husband's shrewd census of the crowd, and knew that no one had noticed what we had done. Everyone was playing a similar game, we were as common as dirt. The realization did not comfort me.

"I think I'll leave now."

"Why don't you yield to temptation, that's the way to overcome it."

Now she was coy, and I was angry. "That's a very old cynic's saw. You mustn't live your life by quotations. Besides, it's not much fun, not for me at least, to yield to illicit temptations. Even less fun to speak like a prig, so . . ."

I had hurt her. Her smile broke apart like a cheap tumbler, shattering; her face changed its set so violently that I listened to hear those inhumanly perfect teeth crack and clink against her shoes. I thought our bizarre encounter had ended, and made no move to rescue it, when the editor unwilling to hear me read aloud my nonexistent book lurched against us.

"Well, well, baby, I see you've been talking to the notorious Jupe. Talk fast, Jupe here is in a rush to find a publisher, just like you, baby. He wanted me to break my date with you and take his manuscript to bed with me. No way, baby, noooo waaaaay." He slipped his arm around her, all the way around, and copped a feel. The girl didn't recoil from him. She was just another jerk.

"I'm late," I said.

"How do you like my Mouse, Jupe baby? A little bit of all right?"

"Listen," I said, "I really dig her. Wow."

She looked at me without rancor. Then she uncoiled herself from the editor as though she were Laocoön and the snakes had fallen asleep. She took my arm and asked me to buy her something to eat. I was at the point of refusing, but I didn't. As we walked away from the editor he fired a few rounds at my back: "Someday, friend, someday . . . arrogant fraud . . . she'll talk your ear off, you poor mug, that's all you'll get off her, an earful of mouth . . . do yourself a favor, baby, don't ever try to get a book published in English, you or your friend, either . . . I've got a long . . . a long . . . long . . . memory."

His words fell harmlessly, so much stray shot muffling around the carpet, and soon we were beyond his range, and the playroom hysterics of the reception were no more than the night cries of some other man's children. Then we were on the street, and I asked her where she wished to eat.

"Some place where real writers hang out."

There was still time to escape. I was in the water, but the surf was only at my waist. I decided to dive. "Are you a celebrity freak?" I couldn't believe I had used that word, *freak.* What the hell was going on? There I was, being led by the gonads into some dank cellar by a toothy, rubbery, perfect thing, there to lie upon a refuse heap of awful words. *Freak!* "Do you hunt celebrities?"

"No, but it excites my appetite to be near creative people. They, you know, make me hungry."

"Maybe cannibalism is your answer, why not eat a novelist up? I know some fat ones, God knows. I'm just a skinny critic, all bone and gristle, you wouldn't care for me."

"Don't say such things, Jupe. I can change your life. Let me. Trust me."

"Look, if it's writers you want, we'd better grab a taxi and get ourselves to Clapper's before all the tables have been booked."

"Oh boy!" I smelled her hair. It was like trees, dead trees, a sawmill, paper, pulp. "Oh boy," she said again, and kissed me; I recognized the smell then, printer's ink; she was a true fan.

Somewhere on the island's Upper East Side is a citadel of vainglory called Clapper's, a tavern where reality is hounded and repulsed by Pomp, Flattery and Expectation. An ordinary bar, really, what in level-headed times was called a joint, or a hangout. Pretty good Italian food is served in one of the Pullman-shaped rooms, the neighborhood isn't fashionable. Electric shuffleboard or Skillpool would fit in fine if the place were what it seems. An old wall telephone rings from time to time with messages for the patrons: shades of Jiggs and Maggie? Not on your life.

Once upon a recent time, using that instrument, a monument to the glory of Western Letters paid out two hundred dollars in nickels, dimes and quarters to speak with another monument to the greater glory of Ditto. The telephonee was at the time cruising the South Pacific. By transocean cable and shore-to-ship the caller roused his friend from his slumber beneath a star-shot velvet sky to tell the happy man his latest novel, the first in a projected tetralogy, had just been *destroyed* on the cover of the *New York Times Book Review*, the roof had fallen in, everyone was laughing, not to worry, the gang at Clapper's hoped he was cruising his ass off, what did the *Times* know about literature?

The saloon had been the *mise en scène* for many another full-screen display of cultural sociology. A half-million-dollar contract had been signed there for the unwritten first novel of a movie actor no one thought was a very good movie actor. After the signing, performed with various pens so that a hard-cover editor, a paperback editor, an agent and a waiter could each have a souvenir, the publisher whose money had been spent asked his celebrated acquisition, "Well, Lance, now that you've got our money, what do you plan to write for us?" And Lance, pushing indignantly away from the table, had answered, "Checks, I'm going to write checks. I don't discuss work in progress."

Well. The Mouse and I threaded our way through some scribblers loitering at the entrance and faced the Traffic Controller. The Traffic Controller was not an employee, he was a hobbyist. He hung around Clapper's serving the place as a jester, the bass note beneath which no other customer could sing, a benchmark of handshaking and name-dropping, living evidence that life could be even less than it was, meaner and more bootless. The principal work of the Traffic Controller was to record every demi-celeb's merest coming and going. Not content to presume to speak to strangers by their first names, he betrayed the confidences of people who didn't even exist: *Marmaduke was telling me the other day about Jissom's publishing company—it's breaking up, gone bust. Jissom told me*

the other day about Spencil's wife, can't get her second novel
published. I hear Spencil's a fag, great people, all of them, really
great . . .

He ignored Mouse. "Jupe, how they hanging? Baby Hughie's here. There he is." He walked a few yards to a nearby table
where Hugh was sitting. "Hey, Hugh, how they hanging?
Jupe's here. I just talked to him." That was it, his work was
done.

I envied him. Really. He had something to believe in, he
shone with a hot light. The Traffic Controller worshiped an
abstract quality, the kind that never disappoints. He worshiped
the half-dozen characters, the pair of syllables that make up a
name, any name; his religion was democratic. Say to the Traffic
Controller that the beautiful girl back in the corner had eyes
for him and hoped that he'd take her home, but forget to
mention her name, and he wouldn't hear you. He'd be whisper-
ing in your ear, *Hey, that reminds me, I saw Norman last week,*
and he looked okay. Or maybe he'd say, *I saw Norman last*
week. All he wanted to say was *I saw Norman,* or maybe just
Norman.

Who was at that moment bearing down on me with a killer
squint, snarling, "I don't know who you are, but my people tell
me you go all over town calling me *Mr. Mailer.* Why don't you
call me Norman, like everyone else on the street?"

"Because I don't know you."

"Exactly. That kind of shit gives me a bad rep. Knock it off."

Mouse liked what she saw. She held my hand. "Thanks for
bringing me. I love this place: I love to watch them let their
hair down, their brains need to cool off. There are at least a
dozen geniuses in this room." She crooked a disdaining finger
at the Traffic Controller. "I don't like him. He isn't serious. He

should chase after movie stars, creative writing isn't show business."

Her contempt reminded me that she was young, and green. Children are purists and tyrants. "You're wrong, Mouse, it is show business, it is. Celebrity, being famous for being famous, that's all your geniuses are after."

"That may be true of others, but not of creative writers. They live forever. Hey, look! What's going on?"

We joined Scharmon. At the next table Baby Hughie was looking through a fact sheet on the novelist Hobey Marvels, whom he was preparing to interview. An area about ten feet square had been marked off by television lights, cameras and cables, and the set resembled a fashion magazine's notion of a writer's aerie. Marvels was at his evident ease sunk in a glove-leather sling chair; at his feet a bearskin rug made from the whole bear—head, claws and raggedy ass—nothing wasted. The author wore a Mexican shirt, unbuttoned to the waist, with puffy sleeves that dripped from his scrawny arms like burst balloons. Around his neck hung a chain of thick gold links, and from this depended a wooden cross with his own agonized figure in cruciform. Hobey Marvels, hottest kid in town. Gothic novels came off his machine fast as he could type. Like McDonald's, he did not want for customers; it was the taste of sawdust and thick relish that drew them. His critical reputation was preposterous: he was taking everyone in, had even taken me in. I didn't even know how it had happened. I had read his most recent catalog of arson, rape, murder, incest, cannibalism and simple bad manners with huge amusement; it was trash, of course, nothing more. But when I came to review the poor thing I offered as truths propositions I could not have believed. I was an accomplice to swelling Marvels' reputation by assuring readers that they were partaking of metaphors for the new anarchies menacing "us": "our" national crimes, "our" illicit longings, "our" etceteras. I claimed the book would instruct by terrifying, when it had in fact caused me to hoot laughter. I said the book, with its rumpus-room ghost stories, would "grip" the reader. I didn't even know what grip meant, or who was the reader. There had been no design to my dishonesty. It was an accident, a freak, a signal to look to my signals. I had thought to repudiate my praise, perhaps in a *mea culpa maxima* revision, a genre much in vogue. But I could never screw up the interest. They used my idle perjury in a couple of ads, then people forgot.

Mouse looked past me at Marvels and said, "I read your beautiful review of his last book. You were so right, don't you worship him?" Then, beneath the table, she grabbed my hot stuff, and left her hand on it.

"Oh . . . yes . . . worship?" was all I could manage. These were risks beyond my wish as well as my need. Scharmon was staring at me. I removed the girl's hand.

Marvels was being dust-jacketed by a top-of-the-line celebrity photographer. The writer's hands were shaking, poor bastard. He had just turned forty, the reviewers were bound to beat his next novel to death. They'd take back their loan of praise with interest, and out of his hide. Marvels had never learned the rules of flattery: he gushed too frankful thanks for the kind things people had said about him, and it embarrassed them that he took their generous attentions to heart. Now he was signing books, and a grip's light lit his face as though it were one of the burning, ghost-ridden houses he liked to describe falling into its foundations. I saw a sad end for the chap. He'd be puzzled by the hostility that fell to his next book *(What did I do differently?)* and wounded by the contempt to be lavished upon the one after that *(What did I do the same?)*.

He'd enter analysis, let a few years pass before he risked another. He'd hone it, read it aloud to his sister and brother-in-law, agree with their judgment that its violent patches were overwrought. He'd resolve to try harder, to do better, and finally he'd find a publisher, not a good one, or enthusiastic. The publisher would market his new book stealthily, as though it were stolen costume jewelry: not worth much, but bristling with risks. The book would be ignored. Marvels would take up trade as a reviewer, but his nastiness would offend readers, and one day he'd get a letter: *Be respectful, smart-pants, if you know so much about novels why haven't you ever written one?* He'd quit literature, and find work doing heroic couplets for a greeting-card company. He'd be drinking by then, and would have changed his name so his colleagues would not know from what heights he had fallen. He needn't have bothered. By then his name would have vanished . . .

But not yet.

"No, no, no! I want you more capricious! There! Yes!"

Marvels didn't seem to like where he was being led. "Really, I'd prefer something more sober, more correct, as though I had high standards."

"Congrats on the subjunctive, dear. Everyone has *standards!* Your pitch is something offbeat and kinky, you know, Hitchcocky. You do want to catch the reader's eye, don't you?"

I tried to be helpful. "Perhaps he could take off his clothes, and you could snap him setting himself on fire?"

"Oh, that's very funny. Hundreds of baggy-pants jokers looking for work and this . . . *amateur* decides to break into comedy. How rigolo. Okay, now, let's go, I've got places to go and people to see, okay Mr. Marvels? Arrogant now, lovely . . . okay, flip . . . ooh, that's sweet . . . ambitious, you're doing beautifully, beautifully, just this last couple of frames, the successful look now, now, now . . . that's it: you're finished."

They were making him up. He grinned through the fleshy paste like a death's-head, nodding at people he thought admired him. Baby Hughie was preparing to begin. The lights came up. They began.

Mouse whispered in my ear, "This is great."

I left to ask the barman for a glass of buttermilk. Scharmon followed me, asked me to buy him a drink, and I did. I paid. The barman brought change. I let it ride while I watched Marvels respond to a thorny question. He knit his mud-caked forehead. "Yes, I guess I'd have to say that drugs are more destructive to the writer's psyche than masturbation, though I haven't written as much about drugs as I might have, have I? I have, on the other hand, written about masturbation . . ."

Just then I heard a cute little jingle, nothing much, the warning bell on a typewriter carriage, the cash register ringing up a small sale, my change falling into Scharmon's pants pocket.

"Scharmon, give me back my money." I held out my hand.

He stared at me. "Jupe, you're far gone. Look at the bar, you poor bastard. I needed change for the phone."

Sure enough, where my three quarters had been there was a dollar bill. People make mistakes.

"I'm sorry."

"No, you aren't. Hey, sport, that Mouse girl—does Kate know her? 'Cause we all do. She's been around, you understand? Everyone's been to the well. You're like last in line, we've been laughing our balls off."

He said more, but I didn't hit him, it was my fault. I wanted to get out, go home, make myself scarce everywhere. I returned to the table to give Mouse money enough to buy herself dinner.

The interview was winding down. Marvels was explaining that Gothic Romance was "realife," that's how he said it, one word. "Just read your daily paper . . ." Hugh was nodding sagely. ". . . sadism and masochism are useful conceits for the fiction of realism . . ."

Enough. I had to say something. "Shut up, you rancid piece of meat! You're idle, you're inept and you're ridiculous."

Before I had said three words Baby Hughie had caused the television lights to blink off, the camera to stop, the mike to go dead. He pointed at me, cocking his thumb like a pistol's hammer.

"Throw the bum out," someone yelled from behind me. "He's drunk."

"No," Hughie said, "he's not drunk, he's just sick with envy."

"Throw him out anyway, he's a wise guy, that's all he's ever been." That was Scharmon, ganging up on me. The bouncer was heading toward me, he owed me fifty dollars from a year ago, he'd have loved to whip my ass, and could have. Mouse was tugging my sleeve. "Let's get out of here, come with me." What was going on? No plain talk allowed anymore? No honor? Had they all gone nuts, did they really believe the horseshit they peddled, did they believe it mattered what Marvels thought about the novel of realism, or about pulling pud? It was one thing to stack fortune's deck on their own behalf when bastard justice glanced away, but for them to believe their own worst lies . . . where, oh where, had the coordinates gone?

I raised my hands to the bouncer, all conciliation I was, no weapons, see? No trouble, let me be. He backed off. I could have left. I couldn't leave it be. One final bit of business, then. I pointed at Baby Hughie. "You know what they call you, chum? The kids? I've heard them, they're not fair. They call you a *pathetic old bore,* how dare they? *An old limp-peckered bloodhound on the scent for a tight young bitch he can't catch. Polonius in hip-huggers,* that's what *I* call you . . ."

"Blow, wise ass, we're sick of you, you're sick, you're not funny anymore."

Hugh was coming at me. I shouted at him: "Nothing's funny, you ignorant tinhorn! It isn't *supposed* to be funny . . ."

"Take off those silly specs, blinky." And then Hugh hit me in the stomach, got off a good shot. I heard money tumble from my pocket, and I thought of the beggar I had shoved a few days before, his money dribbling from his cup. A ring of faces peered down: Hugh, red with rage; Scharmon, curious; Mouse, happy to accept whatever writers in their wisdom wished to act out. I saw the Traffic Controller, heard Clapper calling the cops. Hobey Marvels was writing notes to himself. Hugh bent over to whisper something in my ear—an apology?—and bit me. Someone was shouting at him to get off, I felt wet stuff on my collar, didn't know whether it was Hugh's spit or my blood; Mouse was struck dumb. Then I heard a voice, in clear command, giving orders: "Let him up, be careful of his glasses, don't hurt his hands, leave his hands alone, he's a writer, don't kick his head!"

And while these words were spoken Hugh was flung aside as though by a great wind, and the crowd around me went silent and shuffled off, and I was free to pick myself up and limp away. My savior was not a friend, as I had wistfully hoped, but another: nameless, wearing military khakis, my shadow. Before I could thank him he was gone, a lone ranger indeed.

No one tailed us to her apartment building, a cement block-house a few minutes north and east. It was the kind of address

Big Ten college graduates take when they come East to score. I held a handkerchief to my ear to stanch my blood. In the elevator she said, "I want you to love me."

"Look," I said, "I'm married, you're pretty, more than pretty, you're the best-looking thing I've ever seen, but . . ."

Her gropings were meant to excite. They were what pulp artists call "expert"—mechanical, unregarded, effective.

"Your moves are mighty quick, Mouse, I'm just a boy from Seattle . . ."

She didn't ease off her manipulations. I had a sulfurous vision of her as a lifelike doll, or a male model in drag. I touched her, and she was what she showed, sure enough. I pointed out an odd graffito cut into the elevator's fiberboard panel, beneath the legend ME+ANYONE. It was from Henry James, of all people to show his words on the backside of a linoleum-floored Otis: *The fatal futility of Fact.*

"You put that there?" I asked.

"No, a friend."

I should have run home then, I knew she was a crazy, why did I hang around? The elevator lurched, my heart sank.

Her apartment was a single room. The first impression was of a stage set, dimensions out of register as in false perspective. The play was a monstrosity called *Bohemian Nights* about the Greenwich Village of yore, poets sharing their meager portions, their lovers and their revolutionary verses. On the floor, stage left, was a set-designer's "pallet," a rough bed fashioned from burlap and straw.

She read my thoughts. "I had it built. Isn't it cute?"

Above the pallet a bookcase had been constructed of bricks and unfinished pine boards. Books were jammed at precarious angles, and two deep on every shelf. "There's no title here that anyone would be ashamed to mention in public."

"They are all great books," she agreed, "every one."

At the far corner of the room a private space had been screened off. Mouse explained that it was the work area.

"May I look?"

"No one is allowed there."

The room was a museum of fixations. Here was Comp. Lit. 100 in pix, photographs of Céline, Joyce, Borges, Bellow, Nabokov. There were framed letters from writers even I had never heard of, saying things like *Thanks for your interest in the novel, yours is the only encouraging review I got, even if it was only a letter, thanks for writing it. The book sold almost four hundred copies, here's the autograph you asked for, hang on to it, someday it will be worth a million, heh-heh, if I ever write another book.* There were portraits and busts of the Ancients —Pope, Racine, Virgil, Voltaire, Willie the Bard . . . Cartons of pulp paper littered the floor; I saw ink stains on the walls and furniture, crumpled index cards, broken pencils.

Strangest sight of all: framed on every wall, beautifully crocheted samplers that made the room resemble the quotation page of a second novel.

The Progress of an Artist
IS
A Continual Self-Sacrifice
A Continual Extinction
OF
personality.
by
THOMAS STEARNS ELIOT

I saw Goethe's harsh command shouting through a representation in wool thread of Gothic font: CREATE, ARTIST! DO

NOT TALK! Dostoevsky had come to the party, Leopardi, Gide, the faithful crew, all there. But pride of place, above the false fireplace, fell to Faulkner. The sampler was enormous, the size of a $25 felt banner some freshman might buy to remind himself in orange and black where he was at college. The thing required such brave dimensions because, Faulkner being Faulkner, the aphorism did not suffer from taciturnity. Yonder it hung, and damn the ellipses:

THE WRITER'S ONLY RESPONSIBILITY IS TO HIS ART. HE WILL BE
COMPLETELY RUTHLESS IF HE IS A GOOD ONE. HE HAS A DREAM. IT
ANGUISHES HIM SO MUCH THAT HE MUST GET RID OF IT. HE HAS
NO PEACE UNTIL THEN. EVERYTHING GOES BY THE BOARD: HONOR,
PRIDE, DECENCY, SECURITY, HAPPINESS, ALL, TO GET THE BOOK
WRITTEN. IF A WRITER HAS TO ROB HIS MOTHER, HE WILL NOT
HESITATE: THE ODE ON A GRECIAN URN IS WORTH ANY NUMBER OF
OLD LADIES.

"Isn't it wonderful?" Mouse asked.

"It's a good deal more candid than his *last ding-dong of time, endure/prevail* sentiment. In fact it's accurate, and explains better than I have why I'm heretical. It's the creative artist's declaration of inhumanity. You've invited the wrong man to your shrine, I'm no believer."

"I'll convert you," she promised, coming close. "Let me?"

And so we fell to worship, each according to his faith.

She insisted that the light (another prop, a single bulb dangling unshaded in the defining spirit of the place) be left lit. Before she undressed I still half feared I'd discover no woman at all, but rather a fabrication: plastic and stainless steel, orlon hair, bogus skin stretched across rubber flesh, silicone tits— Vidal's Myra Breckenridge, a type for the times. No such bad luck: she was a woman true to life, with regulation skin and muscle. On her naked breast blazed a saucy birthmark (*cf.* Hawthorne, *op. cit.*), the reassuring legend of her creator, like *Made in Switzerland* stamped on the face of a proper timepiece. She soon commenced to sweat, always one of your happier life signs, and soon I was a busy man, and not unhappy.

True, she was a talker, and between exclamations she delivered herself of fragments from the best that man has thought and uttered, particularly in the way of love scenes from the classics. We sturmed with a will, and then we dranged, while the bookcase above rattled and moaned, and then a paperbacked *Jude the Obscure* tumbled against my laboring butt. I never dropped a stitch till *Seven Pillars of Wisdom* grazed my face and *The Magic Mountain* crashed upon my head and brought our Romantic Movement to an end.

We lay still and, at my urging, silent and in darkness. We were regrouping for a fresh assault on each other when the door opened, and yellow light spilled on us. I tensed, would have shouted at the trespasser, but the Mouse shushed my mouth with her hand and whispered in my battered ear that I was not to worry, it was only her roommate.

The buttinsky walked to the room's far corner, vanished into the work area, and lit a light. ("Why didn't you tell me you live with someone?") I heard pages being turned. ("It doesn't matter. My roomie's a wonderful person.") Sheets of paper were rudely bunched, and the paper balls were hurled against the wood floor. ("It matters to me, I'm too old for these pranks, stop that child, I should leave.") The smell stuck to her: printer's ink, the spirit stink of black ink on high-gloss stock. ("We can do it like this, I'll be quiet, I promise, no one will know.") God's agent! A pen was scratching paper as we worked, slowly at first, then keeping up, driving, a fire storm of writing.

(*"That's* it, baby, oh jesus oh god oh wow oh jupe . . ."*) A reflective silence behind the screen. ("Stop quoting, Mouse. It's just fun, not the Second Coming.") Then, just at the second coming, a typewriter began to clatter, banging away in a clamorous spill of characters, the keys hit so brutally I could picture the paper's deep wounds. I was aghast, and left my own petty consolations to listen. Eight hours earlier I was being translated in a hotel banquet hall. Three hours later I was walking my good lady beneath the window of the Union League Club. Now I was mounted on a perfect stranger (perfect indeed, and stranger than almost anyone), working her will on her, being rained on by Great Books while a girl practiced typing within my naked arm's reach. It was a surfeit.

But not everything, more was coming. For little grunts of satisfaction commenced to issue from the human agent working its infernal machine, and these soon gave way to strapping groans *(Yuh, yuuh, n-i-c-e, s-w-e-e-t, ATTABOY!)* The roommate was no girl. As I live and breathe, a basso.

That was it for me. "Shoo, Jesus, I'm getting out of here, what's the game?"

Mouse laid her finger across her lips. "Shhhh! Don't disturb him, can't you hear, he's having a good session."

"Hey, mister, write your heart out, sorry I plugged your girl, it was all a mistake, believe me . . ."

But the writer was silent. No rustling of paper, no more "Kitten on the Keys." Perfect silence while I tried to dress, to compose myself. I expected him to materialize, bulling through the flimsy screen, strewing paper and wood across the floor. But he did not. The Mouse pouted, and toyed with the broken-spined *Seven Pillars* nesting between her legs. I hunted for one of my shoes, and was at the point of leaving without it when it sailed across the screen. The typing began anew, and soon the groans.

As I crossed the threshold her threat followed me: "Thanks, Jupe, I'll see you soon, I promise, thanks . . ."

The hell you say, like hell you will. The elevator doors swallowed me, I was safe, let muggers do their worst.

8

Kate lay awake, propped up in our bed, reading a novel. My first book lay shut beside her, and I wondered whether she had put it down to take up the novel, and I knew the answer and was jealous. She waved, and smiled, but she didn't look up. She was waiting for me to explain. I couldn't begin. I fetched a glass of water, spring water from Maine, one of my few indulgences. Kate never neglected to order the water, or to put it on ice; she never neglected anything that mattered to me. I was miserable. Well, it had been the first time, would be the last. I returned from the kitchen with my speech prepared: *I corked a girl tonight, don't even know her name, she was pretty, I didn't mean to, it won't happen again, forgive me.* I never spoke the words, they explained nothing; and, at last, I was too decent to confess the truth, what use had she for such self-serving truth?

"I've been in a fight."

She put down the book without marking her place, a sure sign she hadn't been reading it. "I can see that you have. You've become quite a scrapper, haven't you?"

"It was Baby Hughie, that bogus . . ."

"Don't talk about him that way. You're the one who's so proud never to have panned a first novel—'Why heap abuse upon humiliation?' you like to say. 'Poor first novelists,' you say, 'who expects them to do well? Let them sink, I won't shove them under.' What did you expect from Hugh? He's absurd, so what? He isn't exemplary."

"I think he is. Anyway, he whipped me, I think. Hell, strike *think:* he whipped me."

"That's an evil-looking ear, it's bleeding. Come here, let me look. Your glasses are silly, do they work? Can you see me all sharp, and in color? Come here, let me see that ear."

I stood my ground across the bedroom. "He bit me."

She laughed, and so did I. She held out her arms and I went to the bed and sat beside her. She took off my glasses, and fog drifted between us. She tried on my glasses, and I could see her eyes through the lenses, tiny but hard-edged, light beaming through the mist. She was wearing her flannel nightgown, with little yellow flowers I could not see woven through it. She was inviting. My nates were greasy from my session with the Mouse. Kate held out her hand, and I gave her my water glass.

"Thank you, that's nice. And cool." She touched my ear, and I pulled back. "You'll be dead by Monday."

"What do you mean?" I believed in the power of words, believed that spoken prophecies could make things happen. "What do you mean, I'll be dead?" I felt a wisecrack coming, not a catastrophic revelation. "I don't think that was a funny thing to have said, Kate."

"Don't you, really? Ah well, you're the critic around

here, I'll defer to your judgment of what's funny and what isn't. You can die, though, from a human bite. Worse than a cat's, worse than a weasel's. Terrible carrion, think of Hughie's mouth . . ."

"I thought we were obliged to be generous to the young performer."

"Clean your ear. Save your life. Make yourself more appetizing, to me."

I stood above the sink, dabbing at my ear with warm water, stalling. I couldn't bring myself to look at my wound in the glass. Not because I was ashamed, or frightened to see the devil's face stare back at me. Because I couldn't look in any mirror without reflecting on the threadbare device I tripped across every week in my line of work: *He looked in the mirror and saw a man of masculine mien with manly features wearing a powerful nose and sky-blue eyes, two of them, each with pupils. Teeth he had, and a mouth cunningly, shrewdly, practically surrounded by lips . . .*

Kate's hands were folded neatly across the turndown of the clean sheets. She lay in the exact middle of our bed. Her head was cocked, she was looking square at me.

"I'm going to look in on Robin," I told her, stalling. She nodded, but her smile had begun to cramp.

I went to my son's room and looked down at him as if I were Mr. Marine in a World War II novel, taking a last look-round before I shipped out to the Pacific in the penultimate chapter. I felt, that is, like a character to whom something telling was about to happen. Had already happened, how was I to know? Art and life would anticipate each other, I had played with my tin Pirandellos as often as any kid on the block.

The sight of me looming wounded above him startled Robin, and he jerked awake as from a bad dream. The thought of him haunted by nightmares angered me, though I couldn't imagine how or whom to fight on his behalf. I lifted him, and buried my face in his hair, damp from night sweat and smelling like the sea. He lay hot in my arms, and heavy; he was dead asleep again. I whispered to him that I had to go away for a while, that I'd see him soon, "Take care of Mommy." I laid him out again, and smoothed his hair where I had fussed with it, and touched his forehead as a troubled father might, checking for fever. (See *Dombey and Son*—never mind *Dombey and Son*.) I tucked him in tight and he moaned a little, nothing out of the way, and I wanted to comfort him who had so comforted me, to smooth out his wrinkles, to leave him with something. I began talking to him, weaving fantastical tales about people who meant other people well, about novelists who shared their six-figure book club advances with impoverished poets, about critics who said right out: *The book is better than I am, I can't get the hang of it, but that's my fault.* Strangest fable of all, I told of a teacher patient with his students' first stumbling steps, a would-be novelist free of envy and remorse, a true husband, a father willing to let what was be, and give thanks for it. Happy tales, and my son reacted to them as any reader might —with yawns and buzzsaw snores.

"Kate, I'm going north tomorrow morning, first thing, I really am. I'm coming unstuck."

"Isn't that a touch theatrical? Bar fights, I should think, can be cured by steering clear of bars."

I shook my head. I told her I felt awful. She asked who was at fault, pointing at herself, aiming her finger straight at the middle of her face. She had the best face I had ever seen.

"It has nothing to do with you."

"Oh, yes. It has everything to do with me."

"I mean you're not to blame. Please, you know what I mean. Don't you?" She said nothing. "It's my work. And the fads and makeshift . . . I get headaches from the makeshift. My memory's going bad on me, I can't remember much of the time whether I've committed the crime of makeshift myself. I want to do something . . . better. Write something that will last awhile. Maybe a novel, I'm not ruling out fiction. I owe it to you and Robin . . ."

"Oh, Jupe, how dare you! That *you and Robin* line is beneath you, way beneath you, think how it sounds." She waited for me to give in, to call back my words. I did not. So she held up the book beside her, my book. "After all, you've written things before, but never with such talk of *coming unstuck.*" She had lowered her voice to a growl, pulled off an accurate parody of my speech. "And as for this business of writing for the ages, I thought you, of all people, knew better."

There it was, the poor forked thing itself, Jupe. Sane Kate, moderate Jupe. From the beginning I had taught her, and she had come to agree: all the big books were writ, the game was over. No meaner *Moby Dick,* no better *Brothers K,* no greater *Gatsby* would be made. Why? Who knew—it was merely true. Still, incredibly, for the sake of some silly grab-ass at eternal life people would sacrifice secure jobs, loving families, decencies and proportion. A mug's game, sure enough, and how I had come to envy it. Inflated expectations, merest scribbles, unjustified vanity, all of it. And what were the fruits of the game? Nightclub jokes or clumsy word-paintings of objects no man cared to notice, or weather reports or fifth-grade geography projects, or further evidence that man is vile and his work loathsome, shit, the tuff and trass of contemporary letters, The New Novel. Ancient trees were felled to make paper for such nonsense, such stuff as the demented thought was light they had leaked into dark places. The Word. It was absurd, we had agreed, absurd. Not for us to whip ourselves raw racing for the big score. We knew better . . .

Still, I had never imagined that what I had was all there would ever be. I had believed there would be more, something to outlive me, outlive my son. A book. I thought, without articulating the thought, that I would commit a Real Book. An illumination of our age and culture. But who cared about our age and culture? Who could care? Jupe and his times had let each other down, sure as shooting. So the grand act would have to be provoked by another time, another world. Very well, just so there was a grand act, it had never occurred to me there would truly be none, it had never occurred to me that Kate had not expected such an act of me. We didn't talk about it, of course; it had always been there, I had always thought, the thing that glued us. Now I didn't know anymore. Suppose, my God, she had all along taken me for precisely and merely what I seemed, had been as resigned as we pretended to be? Suppose she had meant her words all along?

"Kate?"

"What?"

"Nothing." It was unspeakable. Let Scharmon punish others with his candor, confess to little crimes to divert attention from big ones. I was on my own. "I told Robin a pretty good yarn just now, made it up out of nothing. Do you want to hear some of it?"

"Not really. Your underpants are back to front." I let that pass. "Wear your glasses," she said. "They'll help you with your underpants. Do they help?"

"I'm still blind."

"It's too late, Jupe, for metaphors."

"I know."

"I mean it's too late at night. Wearing your glasses you don't look like a woodsman anymore. Do you remember when we met in sixth grade and you told me your father was a prospector?"

"I said he was a trapper. I'd been reading *Big Red*. I said he was a trapper in the high Sierras near Paradise Lake, Mount Rainier, that I was hanging around school till the snows broke up and I could join him and my dog, Red."

"It wasn't true."

"No."

"Have you lied to me much since then?"

"You know how yore ole Jupe feels about fiction, honey."

"Have you lied to me much since then?"

"No. I have not. Okay?"

"Okay. Come over here."

I slipped into bed beside her and fiddled with the book she had not been reading. *Another, Better World*. What a prodigy we had thought I was! We used to call it *Better World*. Or sometimes just *World*. The nickname saved time, we were rushing then. I threw the book to the floor, threw it gently but heard its binding crack when it hit. Kate shut off her light, and the room went dark except for the throw of my high-intensity reading lamp. It hit Kate's hair like a floodlight, and laid a halo around the top of her head. Her eyes settled on me unblinking from the shadows, and the rest was black. We listened to Robin breathe, an athlete's easy rhythm, a just son's cadence.

"Let me tell you the story I told Robin. It's really pretty good."

"No. Love me. I'm out of love with talk for the time being."

The time being. Present time was the only time she could

ever love. We lay on our sides, facing each other, as close together as we could come. When you loved present time, at least you knew your lover.

Later, just before dawn, I puttered around the apartment, packing. I left money for Kate, more than enough. She would take Robin to Seattle for the summer, they'd make out. I wouldn't take much: my typewriter, some paper, ribbons. Everything else I would need was in Maine. When all was in order I sat beside her and ran my fingers through her hair, just as I had the night before with Robin's. *Honey, there's things a man's gotta do if he's gonna live with hisself. This mornin' they're callin' muh number yonder, and Ah gotta answer. So move aside, lady, and help me strap on muh pens 'n saddle up ole Royal here, and wave me on muh way. 'N iff'n Ah get her done, 'n done right, Ah'll come on home 'n settle down, 'n you've got my word on her. We'll turn this inter the purtiest spread y'ever seed. And we'll raise the young'un here to be deef 'n dumb 'n blind, or leastwise illiterate, so's he won't hafter do like his pa 'n make his woman suffer like his ma done, y'hear?*

"Kate? You asleep? I don't know what's going to happen. I feel pretty screwed up. What do you think?"

She stirred, yawned, sighed happily. Her mouth was fresh. "Do what you always do. Just tell the truth. Say what's what. That's a lot. You'll see, you'll want us up there, I know it."

"Is that all you want? It doesn't seem like enough anymore." She seemed to be sleeping again. The sun had come up. "Kate? I'm leaving now. To beat the rush. I love you."

"Of course it isn't enough, baby. When was it ever enough? Who ever thought it was enough? It's a lot, that's all we ever said."

I kissed her, and left.

Part Two
RETREAT

The sun was getting off a clear shot at me from the left, down near the horizon. To my right clouds were stacked up. Any other day I might have assumed the clouds would run the sun down and blot it out. But today, the day of Jupe's fresh start, I knew it, the sun would take on all comers and burn them off, no contest. The first good omen was the sight of my car, standing where I had parked it and on all four feet, none of them flat. The last time I had left my car near my apartment I had discovered it two days later crouched on its brake drums, no wheels. The time before that, it had vanished into the wilderness of New Jersey.

The great mystery was how the thief had ever got the grudging bastard to come to life. It was a Volvo sedan, four years old, hopeless gray, and when it ran it was a sullen rattler and inventory of practical jokes. I'd been suckered by the ads, had believed that those Swedes and their hard weather and un-paved roads and wintry wits would never let me down. Every piece of prose I read I put on trial for its life, but before the promise of those ads I was as credulous as any rube. *Liberate yourself from the repairman,* they commanded. *Save. Drive it eleven years, or maybe six. Spend your savings on a swimming pool, even a trip to Sweden. We build them to outlast you.*

She was leaning against it, and at her feet was a mountaineer's backpack, jammed full. She was a pretty sight I was sorry to see. I checked the sky: clouds were stalking the sun.

"How did you know this was my car?"

"It had to be yours. The only Volvo on the block. A critic's car, smart money, use your bean . . ."

"Who the hell are you?" I asked her, while I threw my stuff in the trunk. I didn't wait for her reply. "I didn't like playing second banana in your pornographic *tableau vivant* last night. I'd like to forget yesterday, and forget you, so—please—move along, there's a good girl."

"I want to ride to Maine with you. Okay?"

"How do you know where I'm going?" She smirked: *I know what I know.* "Well, sweetheart, I'm a man with plans, and married, so—again, please—fuck off."

She walked away, hefting her oversize tote as though it weighed nothing at all. I looked carefully up and down the half-empty street; the coast was clear.

I lurched and bucked uptown to my office at the university to pick up some getaway swag. I hadn't been to school for almost a month: creative writing courses ended when the reading period began; I was delivered from final exams due to the dabbling character of what I taught; I hadn't honored my office hours since Christmas. My mail slot was stuffed with pleas and rebukes, this and that. Most important, a couple of pay checks and an income-tax rebate that made me blush with shame. The chairman of my department, an old New Critic forever posing replies to literary questions no one of sense would think to raise, had sent me several notes, all of them inviting me to explain myself. The latest was dated that day.

A man who calls himself Fugelman drove me half mad last night, began telephoning at dinnertime, didn't quit till after midnight. Says that unless I sack you my own career will be ruined. Claims friends in high places, principally a couple of investigative reporters, one from *The Wall Street Journal*, the other at *Variety*. Where do you find your colleagues? What the deuce is going on? Some of your students wish to talk with you. One complains that you were "criminally frank" about the unpublishability of his semester novel project. We're paid to be constructively gentle, Jupe, not constructively honest! We've missed your company at departmental lunches. Stop by and see me, it's been too long. Didn't want to bother you at home, or alarm Kate, but soon I must. We've all been hearing queer rumors. You're the innocent victim of gossip, I'm certain. May I help you in some way? I want to support you, of course, but I must see you soon.

Stuffed shirt. I was certain he was a secret voluptuary. Worked *courts-martial* into conversations to demonstrate that he knew it wasn't *court-martials*. Bet your ass he'd support me: I'd probed him once and discovered he couldn't comprehend French or German. I threatened jokingly to write the MLA and unmask him. So, I had him by the *boules*. No: the reason he wanted to support me was that he was a kind man, let so much of the record be in order.

I gave a sweet vicious kick to the books that littered my floor, and watched with repulsion the dust rise from them. I shut my door quietly, and tiptoed past the chairman's office. His door was open—even on Sunday!—and he was at his desk, thinking about Henry James; he did not see me, or pretended not to see me, steal away.

The Volvo stood shaking at the curb, muttering; I never dared shut it off once it agreed to run. Someone, some student, had written a command in the caked grime of the rear window. I had been around a long time, had seen them come and go, and come again. In the beginning they used to finger *WASH ME* on my dusty Ford. Then they painted a Day-Glo *FUCK ME* on my shiny Porsche; then it was ice picks in the paint of the battered Porsche: *TRASH ME!* Now, again, fingered into the filth: *WASH ME.*

I crossed town without a hitch, the Triboro Bridge was a snap, the sun hung out for keeps at Greenwich; the radio was calm, no wars or natural disasters. They collected a toll at Stratford. The day was so bright and I was so on top of it, my glasses sharpening up the edges of all things, that I backhanded my quarter into the basket and didn't wait for the go-ahead light, let them worry about my timing. ("Shot forward" is not precise: "ground ahead" is precise; "inched ahead" is precise.)

There she was at the roadside, sitting on her backpack. I wasn't really surprised. I stopped, let her sit beside me.

She was in high spirits. "What kept you? I've been waiting half an hour."

"Begin at the beginning," I instructed her. "Tell me who you are and what you want. You're hunting me, and I don't know why, I'm not that easy on the eye. But I am a wood-wise old trapper; tell me what the hell you're after or I'll start hunting you."

She said she liked me. I said *Bullshit.* She said my books

enchanted her. I said *Bullshit.* She said she had a hunch I was about to write something important. "Be nice to me," she asked. "I was nice to you last night."

Her hand drifted near my nuts, and I stuffed my foot in the Volvo hard as I could, and whipped it forward. *Jaysus,* it howled, *lay off, enough!* At 60 the valves began to float, the Mouse had her hands back in her lap, and I eased off the throttle.

"How did you get to the tollbooth?"

"I hitched. We passed you. I waved. You didn't look, you were singing to yourself. What were you singing?"

"I can't sing. I'm tone-deaf."

"Like Yeats?"

"No, like Jupe. Just plain tone-deaf, just plain Jupe."

"Tell me about your new book. I know that's why you're going to Maine, to write something special. Will you put me in it?"

"No, it's going to be . . . it's going to say . . . once and for all it's going to . . . I don't want to talk about it."

"What's your favorite novel?" We were crossing the Connecticut River. A couple of white catboats were fencing with each other upriver to our left, toward Essex. The water was plated platinum by the sun. To the right Cornfield Point, and a huge green schooner entering the sanctuary of the river from some high adventure. She wanted to know my favorite novel, she would.

"Well, Mouse, I guess I'd have to say *Buff: A Collie.*"

"The doggie book?"

"By Albert Payson Terhune. The last work of fiction I read with pleasure to its conclusion."

"I hate it."

"Explain yourself, child."

"It's so . . . unserious," she pouted.

"Ahhhhhhh!" I said.

The Volvo moaned at us both.

After a couple of hours of sun-soaked silence we were clear of Providence, and the Mouse sallied forth with a chuckle. "Saying that the way you did made me think how strange human beings are."

"Saying what?"

"What you just said: *Ahhhhhhh!*"

"Ah yes, I see, of course. How strange *are* human beings, after all?"

"Well, when I was hitching to catch you up, I got a ride from a couple of guys in a big black something, a limo."

"Please say 'limousine.'"

"Like one of those, yeah. The car slowed to pick me up. I saw two men sitting up front, I like that, it means I can climb in back alone, no monkeyshines, no hard feelings, that's a pun, *doobel ontondra.*"

I asked her whether she hitch-hiked often, and she gave me a shrewd look: *I get around, my business is my business.* "Go on," I said, "two men up front in a black limousine . . ."

"Well, when they stopped, one of them, the older geezer, creepy-looking, like the uncle in S/M skin flicks, the guy with the pencil-line mustache who keeps a black silk whip coiled in his hip pocket, just in case, this older guy got in back. So I climbed in front with the driver, thought I'd be safer with him, you know? At first everything was jake, like they didn't even ask me where I wanted to go. Not a word out of them, just like you sometimes, no offense, it was real quiet . . ."

"Not like my car, right?"

"Yeah, not like this junker, wow! Anyway, we were just purring along, and I didn't want to disturb the peace or anything, and course I was on the lookout for you. But pretty soon I got bored, and I thought one of them might have a story to tell, I love to hear make-believe of every kind, you know? So I looked over at the driver and, hey, he had this thing in his fist, this boner. And he was tugging at it, driving one-handed. He wasn't even looking at me. His face was all screwed up, like he was thinking hard or something. Driving along, minding his road manners, no herky-jerky stuff with the car, hardly even sweating. The old duffer in back? Same thing, except he was reading *Fortune* while he pumped himself off. Just then we passed you and I said *Look, look at him, he's my fella, look at him singing!* Then *Ahhhh,* then a beat of silence and *AHHHHHHH!* from the back. The driver got stuff on the oil-pressure gauge, the other one tidied himself up on his magazine. Then, down the road a piece they let me out. Never said a word the whole time. Never asked me where I was going, never wished me luck, never even said goodbye. Maybe they were mutes. What do you think?"

"Mouse, I don't know what to tell you, and that's the truth."

"Yeah, it's a puzzlement. Aren't human beings funny, though? I mean, how can you figure it? What was the point of wasting it like they did? I was there, I'm nice to look at, they could have tried. What they did was so . . . abstract. So . . . unreal."

"Just like art," I said. "Just like fiction."

Mouse slept through New Hampshire. The turnpike unwound straight ahead, no quirky curves or confusing forks. Straight on, predictable as gravity, north and east. Then she yawned herself awake, and I pointed to the lobstermen bobbing at anchor in Casco Bay. "A romantic life," she said. "Nonsense," I said. They were being manhandled by a stiff chop, profits were down, it was cold out there. I remembered the heavy stink of diesel fuel and fish and rotten hemp. One summer after school and before college I had spent a seasick summer on a trawler fishing out of Port Angeles. I had been fishing for something to write about. No sooner had I said the words "write about" than the Mouse came alive. It annoyed me that she assumed that I had a Big Book hidden under my hat; it annoyed me almost as much as Kate's assumption that I did not.

I told her a bit about my old man, what it had been like growing up with a confidence artist in sturdy, decent Northwest coast towns. I told her about the time my dad and I were on the lam from creditors and police and finally went to ground on a tiny island in the San Juans. We spent the winter there reading a couple of books a day, talking them out, looking into the rain for The Law. One day a boat poked through the fog, tied up at our jetty, and they took my old man away. I shut up; I was ashamed to have told a stranger, this Mouse, so much about myself.

"Write it," she commanded, insolent as hell. "It's a terrific story."

"What makes you think it's true?"

"What's truth got to do with anything? She was looking at me, puzzled, wondering whether—just perhaps—we were not in fact the conspirators she had taken us to be. "I bet the movies would love it." She was herself again, deferential.

"Movies, my ass! I'll peddle my story to the Ice Capades, watch them waltz through my father's life and mine. Peggy Fleming will be the love interest, we'll have skating bears, skating monkeys, the theme song from *Exodus* . . ."

*   *   *

A few hours down east of Camden we left Route 1 and
poked along a rutted dirt road toward the sea. The tide was out,
I could smell it, we drove toward an honest corruption; not
really different from raw sewage, but the instructed cortex
translated signals of decay into clean flashes: seaweed, salt,
clam-rich mud flats. I was almost home. I would dispose of the
Mouse, somehow. For the moment I was expansive.

"Have you ever wondered how places get named?"

"You mean like New London?"

"No, not obvious places like Los Angeles and Columbus and
St. Augustine. I'm talking about little places, rivers and ponds
and the townships nobody notices. Who bothers to work up a
name for a place nobody will ever notice? How does someone
let the word get out that from now until the end of time one
must call this place Butter Island and the other place Mount
Hoar? Who says, 'Okay, that's what we'll call it if that's what
you want it called'? The place where we're going used to be a
summer retreat for Methodists, they built a boardwalk overlooking the sea and a huge meeting hall, and the house where
I live stands at the end of a promontory that gave the town its
name, Steeple Point—Steeple because the preacher who built
my place tricked it out with a churchy bell tower. Then, after
the First War, when worship fell off in the Methodist line, the
place was sold as a tax dodge to a railroading magnate; he
bought the town, and all its worldly goods, and turned it into
a writers' colony, and named it Pencil Point . . .

"I've heard of it, I'm sure I've heard of it."

The Volvo, aimlessly drifting toward the bushes growing
along the road's untended shoulders, seemed bored, didn't give
a rusty fuck how places get named.

"Oh, in its day everyone managed to get to Pencil Point at

least once every few years to lecture, check out the competition, play a few sets of scandal, you know the kind of thing. But then the great hurricane of '56 blew through, there was a violent tide, the sea receded in the wake of the storm and it never came back. For a while the writers, and the people who lived off them—and the people they lived off—hung around waiting for the water to come home. We could smell it, and the sensitive ones claimed to feel a change in the atmosphere, a fruitful dampness, when the tide ran in. But it never ran in far enough, and the piers began to look absurd standing out from the boardwalk like bridges abandoned after a few weeks' work. Then the beach surrendered to pussy willows, and the wind blew the sand away, and lightning destroyed the steeple that looked like a pencil that gave the town its names. And the writers gave in to a fact of nature, for a change: no sea, no seaside writers' resort. Nothing would lure them back the following summer: free food or free beds or free rides and games at the amusement park. So the railroad magnate sold out to me for a one-stanza song, and I changed its name—here's the point, Mouse—to Point No Point. For good. I got a lawyer to fix it, had a petition signed by all but one of the town's residents, bullied the Coast and Geodetic Survey into marking the hazard Point No Point when they revised their charts a few years ago, just in case the sea should wash in so far that a boat could run aground within a few hundred yards of me. Only one man opposed the name change, the Brigadier, you'll meet him, he's a force to reckon with here in our town. He said my choice of a name gave off weak commercial vibrations, might spook would-be investors. But I prevailed; I cared more than he did . . ."

"Jupe, let me stay with you a little while. I'll help you, do whatever you want."

I thought over her proposal carefully, for maybe five seconds, and told her she could not stay with me. "I've got a rule when I work: no guests, no visitors—not even delivery boys, no one, period."

For some reason she grinned, as though my rejection of her suit had pleased her. "You never let anyone visit, not ever?"

"Never."

"Well, at least you can show me your house, where you work, at least that much?"

"Why do people want to see where writers write? Do you ask bankers to show you the vaults? Are you one of those sad fans who ask *What kind of desk do you use? Contemporary? Traditional? Do you write with a pen or pencil? Hard lead or soft? Do you keep your study at normal room temperature, or do you find it invigorating to write below freezing? Does sex the night before throw off your syntax?*"

"Don't be mean. I don't deserve all that."

I apologized. Drove along what used to be the seafront. Pulled into an abandoned gas station. Groped and hobnobbed while the Volvo grumbled and misfired and whined, a new and passionate note followed by a climb into the red danger quadrant of the temperature gauge. Then the gearshift lever trembled like a whip taut to strike, and we kissed some more, and the car gave up the ghost.

And that was that. Really, that was all that happened. She exhorted me to write my ass off, gave an inspirational send-off: "It won't be easy, no one ever promised it would be easy, you can do it."

The Volvo, all mischief spent, fired up and bubbled along. I drove through the ghost town behind a wave of euphoria, rolled down the window, despite the cold, like some junior high Van Johnson. Cruised past the derelict hotels, past the abandoned saltwater taffy and souvenir stands. To have had Mouse the night before: small potatoes. Not to have banged her tonight, or ever again: there was a big shot for you.

A glass-domed amusement palace had been built at the dead end of Ocean Drive. The Methodists had used its grand interior spaces for band concerts and self-improvement evenings and to agree upon their corporate theologies. The writers on the second wave had used it for poetry readings and self-destruction and to dispute aesthetic theologies. After the sea left, the Brigadier converted the structure into the play palace its architecture called for, and installed beneath its magnificent roof a life-support system for Point No Point: a general store, café and three-bedroom hotel. The Brigadier, a retired staff officer of the Maine National Guard, had grown up among the town's Methodist summer brats, and except in times of war had stuck out the town's desolate winters too. A man of faith, he would hold the town's line till kingdom come. He kept the arcades spotless, and claimed always to sense an improvement in the community's miserable circumstances: once weekenders learned what a clean and decent place Point No Point could be, they'd return, he knew it. In addition to faith and hope, the Brigadier had plenty of dough.

When we entered the penny arcade there were, as usual, no customers, but the place was fully lit, the Brigadier was in uniform, and all hell was breaking loose. It sounded like the climax of a war: churning electric motors, flashing neon, blaring calliope music. A carny barker shouted some incomprehensible shill on an overamplified LP, and a couple of teenaged employees crashed Dodgems into each other. The Brigadier amused himself shooting electric-motivated bears with an electric rifle.

He laid down his arms when he saw us. "Ayup," he said, "you're back. Missus with you? The boy?"

"Not this summer. They've gone West. This is my niece, she'll need a bed tonight, tomorrow she'll be moving on. Can you take care of her?"

"Reckon so." The Brigadier was a little guy, five and a half feet, head in the clouds. He used a clipped down-east accent and a laconic Yankee routine immaculately cultivated for the absent tourists. I gave him free advice every summer, June and September, the same advice: "Why not shut this place? Go to Florida, the Algarve? Open something there, same kind of place, maybe a little smaller, make some money. Your electricity bill must be killing you. Face up to what's what."

"You've got to take the bad times with the good, Jupe. You youngsters don't understand about bad times. I've said her before, I'll say her again—times always improve. A new generation's on the march. Folks'll come back, mark my words, we've got a nice town here, honest people, friendly, willing to lend a hand, no crime . . ."

"The permanent population is five, and they're all members of your family. Get out, this place will bleed you white."

"I'll get by, Jupe, always have. The place amuses me, what's an amusement hall for? You city people always add up the figures in the account book and think you get the right answer. There's more to life than what you call the bottom line. Hell, there's art, this place is like a work of art. Maybe I'm an artist."

The Mouse said she was sure, just by looking at him and his amusement hall, that he was an artist. The Brigadier beamed, nudged me in the ribs, squeezed off a couple of rounds right into the hindquarters bull's-eye of the electric bear, who shrieked and reared up and limped away.

I bought supplies from the man's resigned, puzzled wife.

The Mouse followed me to the Volvo to get her pack, and we kissed goodbye, leaning against the side of the car like a couple of kids home from the hayride, brimming with secrets.

"Are you sorry you met me?" she asked.

"No, I guess not."

"No matter what happens," she said, "never regret having met me. Because of me you'll be famous, wait and see."

"I'll write a Great Novel and dedicate it to you."

"No you won't," she said, "and don't be flip about fame, I'm deadly serious."

"No I won't *what?* No I won't dedicate it to you? Or no I won't write a great novel?"

She evaded my question, kissed me sisterlike on my cheek, admonished me to remember that what the Mouse does, she does for others, and for posterity. She waved goodbye from the doorway. I left her, an eccentric muse backlit by neon in the frame of an old master's eccentric work of art.

No trespassing! signs marked the drive to my house. At the entrance to the point I had installed a cyclone fence; there was a gate secured to iron posts by three stout padlocks. My lights picked out a few more signs, done in Kate's bold letters: cave canem! and point no point viper ranch.

I couldn't screw up sufficient courage to enter the house. Its disorder, so comforting to Kate and Robin and me, was frightening to me alone. The place by night seemed even more absurd than it was: huge, a jigsawman's nightmare, all turrets and gingerbread trim, a swayback stoop, octagonal tower, add-ons run amok, creeping wings. After so long away I was bound to trip across some unpleasant surprise in the dark, a dead raccoon, perhaps not dead, a bird beating against the inside panes of an upstairs window. I sat in the front seat listening to the wind scrape an unpruned branch against the parlor window. The moon was shutting down for the month and when a cloud smothered its feeble light I locked my car doors. The frogs and peepers raising such merry hell when I arrived shut up abruptly when they heard the menacing lock-clicks; I imagined something else had terrified them, and whatever it was had terrified me as well. I imagined someone out there watching me, waiting for me, and I threw on my high-beams and fog lights: they searched a tangle of bushes and vast unfathomable shadows. I blinked them off.

I was cold. Inside the house were blankets, thick Hudson Bay six-points. I wouldn't go in there after them. What was wrong with me? It wasn't like me to let myself be spooked. My night vision was off, true, but I blamed my anxiety on my shadow. My jumpiness was his fault. I hadn't thought about him since I left New York. Where was he now? I thought of my son, frightened the night before and solaced by my little fictions. I tried to tell myself stories, but all I could raise from my fancy were other people's grotesqueries: black comedies, Hobey Marvels' gothics, ghost stories.

I secured the bolts of the Volvo's wing-windows. Buttoned myself deep into my trench coat. Switched on the car's parking lights, to let the world know where I lay, and to take comfort from the kind, dimming green glow of the dashboard. I was very cold now. I would have run the motor to use the heater, but I knew the Volvo had been waiting for just such an opportunity to knock me off with carbon monoxide.

I shivered and dreamt my life through, and because the dream was short and mostly sweet I dreamt it through a few times more. And then it darkened, and I dreamt of books filled with blank pages, of false bindings that hid money or booze, of books unwritten by me. Then I thought of my career as a critic, and dreamt myself into the skin of Gerard David's lying judge, Cambises, the unjust judge. I recalled David's diptych of Cambises, hanging in Bruges. The first painting shows the magistrate stern and intelligent, accustomed to the deference paid him by lesser men. He is under arrest for the crimes he has committed, for his want of mercy. Was I not such a judge? The second panel shows Cambises guyed tight by ropes, stretched out on a table, naked except for a white cloth across his groin, being flayed. People stand nearby. Some of them watch. Others are engrossed in their own affairs, and have lost interest in the several knifemen scrupulously removing Cambises' pale skin. Incisions have been made along his upper arms, and the skin from his left leg has been peeled off as cleanly as a long sock from his knee to his foot. The stern burghers looking down at him are as merciless as he once was: *he deserves what he gets, cut his heart out.* Not a few of the burghers and clerks find his punishment tediously fitting; they seem to stifle yawns.

Would I be similarly skinned alive if I lurched into adult life bearing my own novel? Would they not take off my hide? And yawn as they removed it? It made my nerves sing with pain, yet I could not cease thinking about the crimes of unkindness I had committed, and the crimes that would be committed against me. I lay cramped in the front seat of my automobile, hanging on for dear life till dawn would free me from terror, and perhaps into sleep.

I came awake to chirping birds and the hospitable sight of my house standing where I had left it. I went inside: nothing missing, nothing vandalized, no pipes burst, no plaster fallen. Assuredly, no ghosts. I roamed the huge rooms and climbed the central turret—steeple, pencil, lighthouse, what you will. It was my custom to work in the circular room at its peak, and my first business was to plug in my electric typewriter, compose paper on my workbench, remove the dust cover from my typing chair. After I had thus set up shop I swept the floors, made up a bed, constructed a teepee of twigs and logs in the walk-in fireplace of the drawing room. Then I ate a bowl of canned soup.

I was ready. I took the stairs two at a time to begin work. Every book year had been the same: I'd leave the city with the cuttings and scrapings of nine months' research; three months later I'd return with a book of a hundred thousand words, $\pm$10,000. One thousand words a day. An impressive performance? The fruit of discipline, industry and sacrifice? In fact I wrote five hundred words an hour, and the great part of my days was given over to daydreams and simple indolence. Because I stormed up my own books, and nevertheless enjoyed a reputation for painstaking craft, I thought I had the goods on all wordsworkers. I believed I knew what cakewalks they gave themselves. Labor for them? Half an hour beating the Selectric senseless, and day's work done. A few months of such half-hour days and year's work done. Like me, they'd emerge from retreat wearing pale, harried faces. Writer's pallor, ascribed to the ravages of fierce concentration. I knew better. Did I not know the look of a writer given over to evasion, to naps, to anxiety about prizes and fellowships? Fellowships! What did writers know of fellowship? Lord, I had enough on us all to send us to the chair. My bill of particulars against my fellows would provoke a Senate investigation of critics and mass arrests of romancers. Preparing to make a novel, was I? I should have retired, raised my boy on a wholesome diet of grunts and guitar music, banished language from my life, let the chimps reclaim us. Man, behold his works: the nonfiction novel and lime aerosol lather . . .

Whoa up, Jupe, easy does it. Still a bit tetchy there, no? A man takes a nap now and then, let it go. Dangerous to believe that your own naps are mimetic of everyone else's. No call to curse evolution itself. Besides, a man couldn't climb Parnassus without grabbing some shut-eye from time to time.

After my nap I tried to call Kate, to break the news to her: I Am About to Begin. There was no answer.

I, who had never been intimidated by blank paper, was

ready. Ready. But first: I played three hours of solitaire, practiced my serve at ping-pong till all the balls were lost, composed
lists—of friends (short), enemies (several pages)—the books I
had read, the books I had praised that had gone out of print.
I reckoned my lifetime income, my net worth. I shot pool
against an imaginary hustler (and beat him). I worked up some
monologues, most of them provoked by self-esteem: Jupe as
quarterback, platoon leader, pilot, skipper, climber, movie di-
rector . . . *Go deep; lie low, I'll take out that machine gun; bail
out, that's an order, dammit, I'm going to bring her down on
that beach; we'll never make port before the hurricane hits, I'm
taking her out to sea; stay behind then, I can't let frostbitten feet
stop me, I've got a mountain to climb, I'm climbing it; roll 'em!
cut! print that, Jupe baby, you were perfect . . .*

Then I prayed for a thunderstorm to knock out the electric
power, nothing to be done about it, no more work today, better
turn in and get some rest. But the day was fine, cloudless and
still. So, on with it! But first I took time to clean my typewriter,
dusted its seasick green shell, scrubbed the key heads with a
steel brush, rubbed down the rubber roller with alcohol, blew
into the works, waited for the roller to dry. Then I set my
margins—inch and a half, right and left. I squared up a sheet
of 20-pound bond, and prepared to ambush my first key.

But first I interrupted my work to shut a window; the breeze
might rattle my papers. I was thirsty, or soon would be, so I
went downstairs for water. I noticed the ice trays were not
quite full to the lip, as I liked them, so I refilled them.

I climbed back to my typewriter and stared at it. It stared
back; its quiet motor hummed at me. It was ready.

So I wrote Baby Hughie: "Hey, score that round ten for
Hugh, zip for Jupe, nice fight. Hell, let's forget what happened
at Clapper's. I'm sure you didn't mean what you said, you never

mean what you say. Right? And look, baby, keep your eye on this space, as the billboards used to tell us, keep your eye on me. I'm about to *change the cultural map*, as you used to say in your prosier days. And don't go morbid on us: it's not easy to be a Romantic in an age of skimobiles, progressive income taxes and electric pianos. You give a fair imitation, considering."

Then I wrote my supervisor at Balliol, Sir Alexander C., who had wished me so well and expected so much. I gave him an account of myself during the twelve-year lacuna since my previous letter to him. I wished him good health and a charitable reception for what rumor had it would be a hot-blooded attack on the fragments of Menander, presently to be launched, perhaps. In my haste I inserted the carbons for this letter back to front, so that it can be deciphered only by holding it before a mirror. It runs ten pages, single-spaced elite, and is by intention a fully developed *apologia pro vita mia*, the kind of letter only a chronic suicide could compose. The misbegotten carbon copy was to have served the needs of Kate, Robin and that old backbiter Posterity. It contains an account of my conversion to bitch fiction, and promises that soon, within minutes, I shall set forth upon that Journey my life till now had been a mere provisioning for. I assured the old gentleman that the world had need of a book such as mine—a curious (his favorite word) mix of autobiography, fiction and prophecy—and I even indulged in some market forecasting (I'm sure the boys at Clapper's would understand).

Then I squared the edges of the envelopes with the edges of my desk, and counted them. I multiplied their sum, two, by the postage for both, forty-four, and the result, eighty-eight, made me realize how much I had done with my day. No insubstantial number, eighty-eight. It would make for a huge dinner party; it added up to a respectable lecture audience, an intimidating line of freight cars, more mistresses than I could imagine . . .

Forward: I created my title page.

```
UNTITLED
   a
Work(novel,
     recollection,
     experiment?)
  by
???? (Initials plus
     surname? Christian
     name plus surname?
     Middle name? Should
     I toss in the poor
     bone of a middle
     initial?)
```

No quotation page, no Kafka, Sir Thomas Browne, John the Donne or author of Ecclesiastes, those poor devils who seemed to have written only to work up epigrams for latter-day hacks to pad into novels or compress into titles. I'd let their words rest a day.

I decided to defer a decision on my dedication. Alignments shift.

So: into the Thing Itself. I tried out beginnings in longhand to bring me in closer touch with my words, to feel them cut into paper:

> I begin with the confession that I have not thought about death.

Eureka! I had done it! I was a liar, had written my first fiction.

Trouble was, I didn't get very far. A few black jokes, a few homilies about the vanity of earthly ambition—Kafka and Ecclesiastes after all—and my fingers began to cramp. My eyes, for a change, did not let me down, or did not let me down the usual way. They led me clearly to see my penmanship for what it was, childish and unpracticed, efficient enough for signing checks, otherwise not much use. My pen fell from my grip; my hand hurt. I soaked it in my drinking water, watched it turn whiter than it was, even softer. I wondered whether I had been foolish not to keep a journal. My judgments and prejudices, even more mutable than I had believed, were slipping away from me. Where were my bons mots, now that I needed them? I would begin a journal, it was decided, I would definitely begin a journal. Next New Year's Day I would begin.

An hour later, at dawn, I rapped my typewriter across its keys for good luck, and began my book. I worked the familiar mechanism without effort, the words ran right across the pages with scarcely a hitch. They pleased me, then. I knew that they owed too much to truth for good fiction, yet were not quite true enough. It didn't matter, they represented me fairly:

GROWING up as I did with what is commonly called a pathological liar, I became as a child a critic of fiction, of its manners and consequences. I'll leave the question of pathology to others, but there is no doubt that my father[1] was by habit and temperament a fab-

[1] A Nabokovian warning to the "Viennese delegation" is not amiss. My father was no more to me than any man I might have chanced to grow up with. Sometimes I

ulist. Some called him a confidence man. He invented for himself a variety of histories, different not only in their details but in their contours; none of them—spy, polo player, test pilot, concert pianist—reflected dully upon his wit, his daring or his honor.[2] He was in fact an actor.[3] He re-created his past in part to gain employment otherwise beyond the reach of his qualifications, or to enhance his cultural and credit ratings, or to excite the admiration and envy of gullible tavern cronies. He didn't hold the line at worldly motives when he lied: to ask him the time of day at 5 P.M.[4] was to be told

loved him, sometimes not. But I would never write him up, or down, for therapy's sake, or to snip off his privates. Which are, in any case, mine, to play with or to sell.

[2]Not strictly so. Like Scharmon, though with a world more invention and propriety, he might tease himself with some insignificant—and need I add fictional?—failing. He would often, for instance, censure himself for excessive generosity: *I'm foolish, I know, but what can I do? I love to help others.*

[3]He was not. He was by profession a schoolteacher, and history, for God's sake, was his game! He was a relentless gossip, and false conclusions drawn from simple facts were his specialty. He propagandized on behalf of King Richard Crookback, with whom he claimed blood kinship.

[4]I don't know why I use this conceit to illustrate his procedure. Because he in fact prided himself on knowing and giving the correct time of day. And why 5 P.M.? Why not 6? Or the more euphonious eight o'clock. Five pee em grates; I should have done better.

that it was 4:55 or 5:05. My father had the designs of a natural artist: he created his own temporality and circumstances, wrote the part he chose to play and then walked as lead man upon a stage he had devised and fabricated.[5]

Today I judge his grand failure to have been one of aesthetic rather than moral impropriety.[6] But when I was a child, at a time when fantasy should have been a hobby and a solace,[7] I began to measure fiction by ethic's rules. Surely, I told myself, it was wrong to tell tales.[8] Surely it was wrong to steal knowledge from another by concealing a truth —time of day, for example—from him? Schoolboy life, in which simple speech and transparent motives were most highly esteemed, nourished in me an unhealthy appetite for accuracy. Getting things right, telling the correct time and date, fixing a place on a map: these were precisions that became for me fundamental. They enhanced my character, but left the armory of a would-be writer poorly provisioned. I continued to read fiction, but my affection for it became wary, complicated

[5]The play here on fabricate—*to make, to fake*— is sufficiently inventive to discharge the offense immediately above.
[6]Today indeed! It had just that moment stolen into my mind, and I wrote it before I had taught myself to believe it.
[7]And probably was.
[8]Surely, I assure myself, I could not have been such a prig?

by my conviction that a lie was a lie,[9] however elegantly it might be told. I could live happily enough with technical experiments and Gothic extravaganzas, but I was offended by fiction that refused to announce its artifice, advertising itself as history or autobiography.[10] I once said—and seemed to mean —that I'd rather be Edmund Wilson than Scott Fitzgerald, that I'd rather write the truth about *The Great Gatsby* than write *The Great Gatsby*.[11]

I became what I fancied.[12] I imagine my name is known to most of my readers,[13] but probably as a critic and lecturer. Now I leave that behind. Changing what I find, making it over,

---

[9]This is *news?*

[10]!!!!

[11]Well, yes. Right off, you see, I saw I had the knack for criticism. I refused to take anything on trust, wouldn't believe that things were what their surfaces made them seem. I was forever catching school chums out on matters of fact, correcting their errors in regard to batting averages, the fastest beast afoot, the coldest place on earth, the name of the losing clan at the Glencoe Massacre. I was an adroit syntactical mechanic, could tear down a sentence and grind its valves and rebuild its pipes and joints. The Volvo, life, defeats me.

[12]One of a dreamer's more common hazards. Not as good as Wilson, of course, but good, almost good enough.

[13]I don't know what I meant this to mean. On the literal level the statement is true, but tautological, since the reader would know my name from the would-be book's title page long before stumbling across this frosty sentence. On any level other than the literal, it is a breathtaking presumption.

bending straight lines—these are now my daily enterprises.[14]

So, my conversion from a foot soldier marching with the fact-seekers' infantry to a knight-errant of artifice[15] was gradual. I experienced no Damascus[16] but returned instead to instinct and my father's legacy. The philosopher[17] asks: Does some power, or even virtue, reside in truth that is denied to falsehood? And the philosopher now replies: Depends on the falsehood. My father's fictions, for instance, were unworthy of his imagination.[18] He robbed the substantial world of its clichés in order to dress up his impostures, but he failed to replenish its diminishing store of dreams.[19] His shabby conjuries finally wore him down, and his exhausted imagination refused to support his needs, and barflies and credit managers saw through his thinning costumes to a scarecrow's broomstick skeleton and straw stuff-

[14]Well, one day at least, *that* day.
[15]Oh, come off it!
[16]I love that word, *Damascus*. Exotic, musical. And the rhetorical tactic of letting a single word, meaningful only to a man who knows his Gospels, stand for such a grand concept as conversion appeals to the snob in me. It's clubby, I know, a low vice of High Tables, but it's fun. Of course my true Damascus was most likely a piece of the Mouse's ass.
[17]That's me.
[18]If you look sharp, you'll see that this doesn't really scan, since the only evidence I ever had of his imaginative resources was by way of his fictions.
[19]Who knows about these things?

ing, and he trailed away, wondering whatever
had gone wrong. And then, one day, he stopped
lying. Owned up to what he was, poor devil, and
now he's nothing at all.[20]

I will not end like him,[21] and that is why I'm
writing this book. I undertake here and now to
break free of the gravitational pull of
earthbound facts, to legitimize my yearning
to talk bullshit, to shed my clumsy loads of
personal history, to declare myself unin-
vented, to invent myself, to soar . . .[22]

[20]Who am I to judge?
[21]No comment.
[22]Here the narrative breaks off, interrupted in
mid-ecstasy, abandoned now forever.

The catastrophe scene of *Don Giovanni:* a magically abrupt eruption of weather. I had been reading aloud while I composed, shouting my words at the silent house (*to invent myself, to soar* . . . stretching those last two syllables out to heaven), when hailstones began to pound against the roof. I looked outside and saw, miraculous June sight, the world going white; the sun was snuffed by the great fall of stones, and I could only with difficulty make out the Volvo, now translated into an inoffensive hump of ice.

The hail beat against my windows till I thought the glass would break. From far off thunder boomed, and lightning snaked through the curdled sky. The fireplace began a nasty hiss and downstairs I discovered chunks of ice as big as plums falling down the chimney. Trying to close the flue, I burned a couple of fingers on my best typing hand. The ice was melting, guttering the sodden embers now beginning to smoke. The smoke spread through the drawing room, stinking, creeping like a dismal, hopeless stain through all the lower rooms. It was a tossup whether the most menacing Gothic effects hung outside my house or within. I was prepared to flee into the storm when I saw him, standing in my doorway, tilting casually against the jamb, grinning.

"Good afternoon, sir. I believe you recognize me?"

"Yes. Who are you?"

"That will take a lot of our time. For now . . ."

"For now, get out of my house!"

"For now, sir, I think I'd better open that flue."

He spoke softly and precisely, like me. He walked to the fireplace, and I moved aside to let him pass. I already knew that were I to stand my ground between him and any place he wanted to be he would raze me, and walk on me. He wore gloves of soft chocolate calf, and in contrast to the rest of his outfit they were elegant, and they frightened me. He opened the flue, and the smoke was sucked up the chimney, and he smiled, and as the malign fog cleared I began to see him more acutely. He was cut clean, aerodynamically beyond reproach, a Hitler Youth by his short-cropped hair and his costume. He had designed himself for speed and utility, wore sturdy boots and that khaki jacket with pockets aplenty for pencils, notebooks, knives. I walked to my front door to escape him, tried the door, shook it; it was locked, of course.

"What do you want?" I asked.

He shook his head, the same sad gesture that had enraged me at the symposium. "I've been worried about you, sir. Ever since your crazy lecture the other day I've been *really* worried about you. Especially after your friends worked you over at Clapper's. I know how that kind of session can smart. How are you? Better? Calmer? Your tough old self again?"

He invited me to sit, in my own goddamned house! I stood.
"I know you, don't I?" I was stalling for time while I collected
my wits. I was mindful of the possibility that he was no one
at all, that he was no more than a distasteful mess of fancies
cooked up by an overheated imagination in a smoke-choked
room during a hailstorm out of season, the product of solitude
and obsession. "There's something about you . . ."

"Think hard, sir, I'll come back to you." He smiled, but his
voice was not friendly. "Long ago, years and years. Ignore what
I look like now, Professor, use your imagination."

"Of course." It was the word *Professor* that brought him
back to me. His name was gone, didn't matter, something with
too many consonants, Central or Eastern European. I had
taught him creative writing back in the odd old days when I
was a fire-breathing missionary self-sent to preach things-of-
beauty-that-forever-endure among the Hottentots. What a
worshiper I was! What an ass! Yes, I remembered him well
enough. The Beats had been in the saddle then, and he had
affected a Bohemian countenance. I recollected clumps of
damp, wiry hair sprouting from his nostrils and earholes. He
was a bearded thing, foul-smelling, forever popping off in class,
quick on his Keats. Had moist eyes, sad and rheumy. Now his
nose and ears had been barbered, like his chin, and his eyes
shone dry and hot. Before, his mouth used to drizzle, leaking
vaporous sentiments about immortality, the sacred psyche,
higher purpose, the usual. I had him through an entire aca-
demic year. He talked too loud then, now too soft. Then he
shouted, insinuated, whined, intruded, quoted, stammered
with excitement, begged. He enjoyed none of the reticence by
which we recognize our fellows in sanity and civility. He had
done something absurd, something that had infuriated me,

what was it? Ah, of course. It was the custom in the university's creative writing courses to mimeograph the week's run of fabulations several days before each class met, so that students as well as their teacher could work up a brief against them. The trespasser now kneading his cat-man's gloves would not yield to this convention. "You're the one who wouldn't submit stories in writing, who would only read them aloud. Right?"

"Well done, Maestro, you remember. I was afraid the other writers would steal my ideas, or my style."

"You were afraid I'd steal your stuff. Admit it."

He dismissed me with a cutting gesture of his hand. "It doesn't matter now. Who cares? And don't call my work *stuff.*"

Yes, he had been touchy then, too. I understood his classmates to call him Weeper, because he would sob at the climaxes of his own stories. And he would weep as he brought the news, hot from the library basement, that artists suffered: he would tell us of Dostoevsky in front of the firing squad, of Malcolm Lowry drunk and dishonored and set upon by wild dogs. He would recall the legendary suicides: Mayakovsky, Hart Crane, Hemingway, Pavese, Woolf. His classmates laughed at him openly, and hated him. Ah, more was coming back. "They did something to you, didn't they? I remember now. The kids terrorized you."

"I suffered for my art. You taught us to endure."

They had ambushed him in the library, outside a lavatory stall where his practices had caused him to be named not Weeper, as I had thought, but Whipper, Jack the Whipper. They had caught him with back issues of *Evergreen Review* whose advance-guard photographs of the human body *in extremis* offended their notion of decorum. They had debagged him, and painted on his naked lower region the names of pop writers, Margaret Mitchell, Irving Stone, Ayn Rand. They stole his trousers and pants, and in the scuffle cut his mouth and broke his nose, even now turned slightly left from full face, ten degrees out of register. He was hospitalized for a couple of days, would not bring charges against the thugs. *The true artist is always a victim of the mob.* That's what he said. When the class next met I asked the bullies why they had done it. They wouldn't answer, but I thought I could guess: his stories were false, fancy, overwrought, persistent, long. He smelled awful. His tears were sudden and frequent. There was no excuse for what had been done to him, and I feared that my own distaste for the boy had provoked the crime against him. When he came out of the hospital he called on me at my office. *Why must the artist and his society remain at war, Maestro?* (That's what he chose to call me, who was I to correct an injured man's locutions?) He sat there, pointing his swollen, bearded face at me, his forehead glazed with subway grime, weeping on my blotter. I tried to let him down gently. *Well, son, I think perhaps your intensity makes these particular readers uncomfortable. Perhaps you could loosen up, perhaps . . .* But as usual he interrupted my civilities: *No half measures in art, Maestro, you've taught me, I only practice your preachments. And what about you? Don't think I haven't noticed, you hate me too. Why? I love you and I love the work you teach. Why won't you love me back?* Jesus. What was I supposed to say? I sighed. I stared out my window. I thanked God for the gift of accurate navigational instruments to tell me where I was, and what, to keep me off the killer reefs upon which he had come hard aground. I looked at his face. Then, sighing again, I injured him: *Why should I like you? Where is it written that we must like one another? I teach standards, not love. The light that blinds is the light for me. No, I don't like you. What does that have to do with anything important?*

Now I sat beside the cold fire, listening to thunder explode, looking him over after all those years. He noticed me stare at his gloves and blushed, as though I had caught him at some mischief. He removed the glove from his right hand and I was surprised to find it covered with tiny tattoos: a mess of words and characters, like a scratch sheet left too long beside the telephone. He held it close to my face and I identified the doodles as proofreader's marks, and reminders about grammar and spelling: *i before e except after c; NO JARGON! effect and affect—careful!* He had the smell of the inkhorn about him, as repugnant to me as it was familiar.

"Cute idea, isn't it, Maestro?" He didn't smile. I nodded. He replaced his glove, balling his fist several times to relax his fingers.

Before he was set upon by his peers his tales had been stocked with dwarfs and magicians. Every object stood for another object, the second invariably less interesting than the first. The stories came equipped with thoughts only Germans could have thought, about the oneness of everything and the everythingness of one. But after the humiliation and after our talk his fiction changed course. His next story was short and sour; it clinked true, like a silver coin struck against crystal. The hero—Weeper or his mouthpiece—sits at his desk composing a short story for creative writing class. His roommate appears in the doorway and shouts *Stick 'em up! I've got you covered!* The (fictional?) writer hero writes on, mutters *Leave me be, go 'way, I'm creating.* The roomie says *You're done for, punk,* and blasts the (fictional?) writer with a water pistol filled with ink. The ink seeps into the hero's shirtback. It defaces the page he has laboriously elaborated with words. The (fictional?) writer reaches into his desk drawer, removes a Colt Python .357 Magnum and drills his roommate in the belly, one shot. *I warned you: never disturb me when I am creating.* The room-mate miraculously survives, and understands at last the gravity of invention.

"You wrote the thing about the gunslinging wordman, didn't you?"

He replied with another slicing gesture. Not from modesty, but from the putative prominence of an adult who has put aside his toys. "You called it a great story."

"Well, it was pretty good, deft, not bad. But look, however tempting it is to summon up old times, I'm afraid I'm busy just now. I've got my own work, you see; this is my time in the desert. Alone. Even disinvited my wife and boy this year. So, while I hate to throw an old student on the mercies of a tempest, I'll have to . . ."

"No. You didn't say my story was *pretty good,* or that it was *deft.* You didn't shovel such reviewers' horseshit at it. You said it was *great*—period—*great!*"

"Come off it. That year I told everyone his story was great."

True enough. I played the anarchist that year, made mischief. I had met privately with each of my students, and told each in his turn that he, he alone among his fellows, gave off a whiff of genius. A nasty crime, I'll confess it. But it was a hard time for me. (So what?) Even then I had sensed what was ahead, that I would live out my life as a spoiler and a scourge (good prophet), that my name would outlive my body by no more than three weeks, if I was lucky. So I punished the whippersnappers by teasing them into their own feeding frenzies. Ugly.

"Maybe you boosted the others, too. I don't care about that. You meant what you told me. I know it. I believed you."

"I didn't mean it."

"Everything I've done since that day I've done because of

what you told me about myself. Maybe the story wasn't great, not in a class with Chekhov's or Hawthorne's. But you saw into my depths, and called out my voice. I know you don't lie. I've followed you carefully, believe me. I've read every word you've written since you told me I was a great writer. Every word. You're a truthteller, a man who knows talent. You told me what to become, and I became it."

He never blinked. He bobbed his head to keep me dead in his sights, just like a snake. Do snakes blink? I must have read about them somewhere, books have brought me nothing but trouble. Books and writers. The hail beat down, advertising the world's end. I regarded my visitor, clasped my hands behind my neck like a professor, tried to seem relaxed. But I was trembling violently, and my masquerade was betrayed. "Well, since you're here, you might as well say what brought you. What do you want from me?"

"Everything, Professor. You can do so much, so much. Just like before. I knew you'd help."

What had I ever done for him? I had lied to him, and let him work me over with questions after class: *Pica or elite, which made the better impression? How about paper stock? What weight? Twenty-five percent cotton too heavy, too pushy for a beginner? Should typescripts be paginated top right, left or center? What were North American serial rights? Who owned them? What was a fair split, subsidiary-rightswise?* He had pestered me to recommend him for a grant: *Don't hold back, Maestro, show them my best side.* What best side? What had I written? *The day this lad deserves a fellowship I'll be in Stockholm picking up my Nobel.* The lad got his money, but I've never been to Sweden.

"Who said anything about helping? I didn't say I'd help you."

"But you will, wait and see. You'll never regret it," he added as an afterthought. He was a cool customer.

"What's your name again?"

"Never mind my given names, Professor. I've forsworn them. It's absurd for a fabulist to drag through his career names some idiot happened to unload on him. A character's names are important words. I made up my own name."

"And what is it?"

"I call myself Man of Letters. Like it? There's negative capability for you. Have I not shed the luggage of personality, as the poet commanded? Are the decks not cleared for artifice? Away with human parents, with names and birthplaces. The Man of Letters: what I am, what I do. Stupid people laugh when I introduce myself. I don't care. They call me Mole. Let them." He waited for me to say something. I didn't know what to say. He continued, his excitement now tightly reined: "Mole suits me too, I guess. I'm that sometimes, the way I hole up, burrow in, focus on things inches from my nose, squint the way you squinted before you got your glasses. You can call me Man o' Letters, or Mole, whichever you prefer."

I removed my glasses, and the creature disappeared into a soft wave of fog. I was encouraged, regained the snap in my voice. "Well, Mole, on with it, what do you think you want from me."

"I don't know where to begin—"

I interrupted him then. Looking back, I see that it was my first grave error, unleashing my fury: "You presumptuous nit! How dare you break in on a serious man, follow him for half a year and more, disrupt his work, make mock of his privacy and a misery of his reputation. How dare you say you *don't know where to begin* when he asks for an explanation!"

"It goes better the other way, sir: mock of your reputation

and a misery of your privacy. That's how I'd write it, though I'm not certain *misery* would sneak past my blue pencil." He was disappointed in me, waited for me to see the light. "Don't you agree, sir?"

"Have you written a book, son?"

"Yes, sir."

"A novel?"

"Yes, sir. Well, no, sir. I mean, not exactly a novel, not merely a novel. It's got verse in it, and philosophy, and true facts. I don't know, I can't really describe it. But when you read it—"

"Whoa up, whoa up there! When *one* reads it, I think you mean to say." He tugged at his forelock, and I was fool enough to believe I had him on the run. "I'll give you the names and addresses of several publishers. What the hell, I'll even give you their home phone numbers, too. Then you must leave this place." I rose to fetch my address book, and he jumped toward me. The move frightened me, and I stood still.

"I was taught to rise when a master rises, or enters a room. Forgive me. Please sit down. I don't need their names or addresses. They won't accept my book, the ignorant bastards." He swore at them more in pity than in heat.

"So what else is new? Publishers reject books. Sometimes they're wrong, mostly they're right. Perhaps you should—"

"Perhaps, Maestro, you should shut up. Don't fob off that tired lecture on me. Serve it to the others, hacks and mendicants, but not to me. *Have patience, write other books, times are bad, money is short; publishers are decent, read every script they're sent; take your time, nurture your career, a good book finds its audience* . . . like that?"

"Something like that," I confessed.

"When I tell you they won't accept it, I mean just that: the mail clerks refuse to take delivery of my book."

"But that's nonsense." His face tightened; he didn't wish to be accused of nonsense. "Why won't they accept it?"

"They say it's too . . . much."

"How long is it, how many words?"

"Fifteen cartons, fifteen beer cases."

"Sweet Jesus!"

"And they won't take manuscripts written in longhand, especially pencil."

"Quite so. You can't expect anyone to read a book in such a sorry state."

"Of course I can. I expect you to read it."

"Too much, son. You're asking me to give you a week of my life to—"

"It will take you at least three weeks to read it through properly."

"You must be crazy . . ."

"It has cost me the best years of my life. Your advice cost me the best years of my life. I don't blame you: you were right to alert me to my gifts. But you can't expect to scatter your words all over the place, planting them in my dreams, and have nothing come of them. Words count. You spoke: big talk, tall words. Now deliver. You sowed the goddamned wind, Maestro, now we'll reap us some whirlwinds. Do you follow me?"

"I understand. I understand you can stuff your book—and my words, if they'll have you—plumb up your bunghole. I wouldn't look at your silly excretions if somebody stuck a gun in my face . . ."

"Someone just did." And so he had. Colt Python, as I hoped to live, hoped to breathe. "Now help me lug in my gear from outside. It's time to settle down to business."

We've been like this a week now. His gun at my head while I try to read his crabbed scrivenings. He sits across my desk from me sunup to sundown, watching me; today he knifed his title into the glossy walnut surface: THE MAN OF LETTERS. A few minutes ago he offered me two hours from each working day to write for myself. I'll keep this journal; serious work is not possible in such circumstances.

"Why do you point the heater at me all day?"

"It's for your own good, to get you off the dime and keep you going. You told us once in class that your worst vice was procrastination, remember?"

"No. Besides, that was years ago. I've been working my ass off for you—eight days now, isn't it?"

"Just so. You see: the gun helps."

*   *   *

He knows his work too well. He recollects precisely where his jokes are buried, and he scowls when I pass them by without visible reaction. When I fail to smile or to nod at his sagacity, his trigger-finger cramps and I shake in my slippers. Trouble is, I can't decipher his chicken scratches without enthusiasm-robbing labor. Until the final forty or so pages he used a soft-lead pencil and wrote on onionskin. He will not tolerate the tyranny of lined paper, so his sentences wander off the horizontal. My hands are always filthy, and I leave fingerprints and smudges on his pages, and he warns me, several times each day, to treat them more respectfully, and keep them clean.

His spelling is capricious. On a single page he managed to commit *babmitten* and *chesterdrawers*. But I must confess it, some of his sentences sing.

He's in luck: I'm loaded with cash. Otherwise he had calculated every move and prepared for every contingency. He forced me to telephone the Brigadier and tell him my secretary and ex-student was living with me and would tend to my necessaries while I communed with my Muse. That this selfless fellow would call for mail and food twice a week. That I was to be left entirely in peace with myself and my manservant. The Brigadier, credulous sod, swallowed this preposterous fiction without salt.

Kate called from Seattle the day after this Mole (now oiling his revolver) stole into my life. She was so sound, so clear, so free of confusions that I thought my heart would break to hear her. I talked on the drawing room phone and Mole, within easy range, listened on the kitchen extension. He made me rehearse

· 142 ·

with him what I would say. I was permitted to express reserved affection. I was not to complain. I could wish, coolly, that she was with me. She phoned again this afternoon, two weeks later, to tell me my father is dying. Would I fly to Seattle to take charge and see him out? I begged the Mole with my eyes to let me go, and he shook his head. I hesitated; there were limits.

"Are you okay?" she asked.

"I guess so," I said. He nodded his spouting conductor's wand at me. "Sure, I'm fine, really."

I told her I was sorry, but I'd have to stay put, that my work was coming along too nicely to interrupt it. That must have been message enough to her that I'm in trouble. She can't believe I'm such a prick?

He stands when I enter a room where he's been sitting, and he calls me "sir" or "professor" or "maestro." This morning he added "Meistersinger" to his collection of honorifics. Just now he dredged up from the stinking bowels of his knapsack a dog-eared leather-bound notebook chock-a-block with bons mots I had wing shot years ago in his class. His adulation once made my guts roil. Now I have become oddly dependent on his deference, for it's the solitary index of my value to the world described within these walls.

I think continually of escape. But he never slips, and never really sleeps, and before he goes groggy he always locks me in one room or another. Why doesn't the Brigadier suspect something? The Mole orders such repellent food, why doesn't that tip off the old soldier? Where are you, trespassers? Where are you, Jupe? How quickly everything vanishes except the one thing stuck under my nose. To be able to shut out the world out there: the great reader's great virtue, my greatest vice. I'm beginning to respond to this monster as though he were human. He's all I've got, for the time being.

When I praise some conceit that he invented he calls me a "genius," a "great critic." Truth to tell, I don't know what to think of the thing I'm reading. Despite my expectations, he has wit and grace. He has also stolen me blind. I find my own spare parts—battered hub caps and a tarnished radiator ornament—attached to his cumbersome vehicle. I'm in a bind: he knows I'm following my own spoor through his work, so he knows that I must enjoy much of what I read. Yet I'm terrified to encourage him. Suppose he dreams up new ways for me to help him?

Kate just hung up. My father is dead. He escaped from the clinic where they were keeping him more or less alive. Bribed a nurse with a rubber check. Rented the Lewis & Clark Suite at the Olympic and passed to the other shore in the company of a pick-of-the-litter pross. The girl was a sport, content to have been had on the house, but the hotel's mouthpiece wants money for the rooms and for a mattress soaked through with its own Pol Roger. Kate ordered me West for the funeral. I knew what I was obliged to tell her; the Mole didn't have to prompt me. We've been together less than a month, but sometimes I feel less like his victim than his accomplice.

"I can't, Kate. The book is too important. Believe me."

"What the hell is going on? Are you one of the bad guys? Are you suddenly a capital *W* Writer? This is what's called a crisis situation, husband, father, son. Now get on out here."

"It isn't that simple."

"It's just that simple. Is there someone with you?" He thumbed back the hammer of the equalizer to half-cock, and the click made me jump. "Answer me, Jupe. Are you alone?"

"I'm a prisoner, call me a prisoner of my work. I love you—"

"Shut up. Words don't count, words don't matter at all."

"But they do."

"Not to me. If you love me, come West."

"I can't. You see . . ." But before I could tell her what to see, she had hung up.

Today I know what recently I've feared. The Mouse clapped me. Leaky, rusty faucet, frequent and painful urination, quite frequent, very painful. My sweet Kate, can I make you understand?

I've finished his book. As I feared, he wants me to talk about it. "Tell me what you really think."

"I think you should put it in your bottom desk drawer—"

"I know, I know, I've heard it before. Put it away for a few months and—"

"I didn't say that. Put it in your bottom desk drawer, and lock the drawer, and then set fire to your desk. It won't fly. It suffers from irregular usage, terminal chaos and illegibility."

"That's all right, sir. You'll just have to read it through again. Pretty soon you'll get the drift, and then you'll love it."

"But we've been at this five weeks!"

"And hasn't the time flown?"

Some pickings:

1) "Why do we create? A composer makes signals for the performance of music he will never hear performed. We are told that cave painters in the Dordogne crawled through mud and cut their bare legs on stones merely to scratch a few crude strokes against limestone, to create a vague simulacrum of a

tusked and furry predator. I have given my best years to this (readerless?) book. Why do we continue?"

(I'd bet my hat that Mole, blind in his burrow, couldn't tell me whether "Dordogne" is a place, an era, or a cut of veal. As for "simulacrum," it's one of my favorites; he stole it from me, stole the cadence of the passage, too.)

2) "Why should readers honor me? My rules are not theirs. I have no use for the present, other than the use to which a lens-grinder puts sand. I despise Common Man. I freely confess that I have grand pretensions. No lowest denominator for me. And while I'm a royalist, so am I an anarchist who celebrates, for the purposes of my work, the subversive, the irrational, the scandalous, the irrational, the criminal. In this novel I create a man, verb him into a semblance of life; then I dialogue him into a terminal disease. I shoot him through with words and leave him dying, unattended, for many pages. Then, cool as can be, I blow him away, erase him. I am a murderer."

(The making of a bit of once-upon-a-time is no consequential act, has not been for a long time. It's a game.)

3) "Fiction is a game that obsesses me. The novel is not dead, any more than the short story is dead . . ."

(Any more than his character is dead, truly *dead*. Very well, then: writers are at play, but their opponents the readers have run home for supper. Leaving the Mole to play with himself.)

4) "What a high price we pay to commit art! Literature must be the most dangerous of occupations; it surely has the highest mortality rate. Suicide is the common end of writers. For those willing to endure, the portion is poverty and anonymity. Death would be preferable to anonymity. Suicide *is* a way to the goal. So is murder?"

(What a cute stunt! Tipping off the reader to a forthcoming self-destruct so the reader may believe himself the most envied of all voyeurs, the-last-to-see-him-alive. Mole is a babe in the woods, truly. The foolproof bid for a reader's sympathy is the terminal acknowledgment page, thus: *To my editor, with apologies and in gratitude. Apologies for the interruption of my work while I lay stricken. Gratitude for the visits he paid me while the outcome of my radiation therapy was less certain than it is today. I wish my work were better. I would like to believe that had God made me better, my work would also be. I thank God for having made me at all, for however brief an earthly lease. Now I must face His judgment, since I will so soon leave forever the jurisdiction of my secular judges, you, my patient readers. You must try me* in absentia: *may you temper justice with mercy. And don't forget money.* The Mole suffer? The Mole weep of death? If I told him that prose make-believe caused cancer of the finger he'd burn his pencils before lunch an hour hence.)

5) "Only a simpleton or a cynic would deny that strange powers inhabit the creator. I make someone up, bestow a name on him, an address, an occupation. Where does he come from? I ask myself. An immaculate conception? I hook up the wires that connect my fingers to his vital systems. At first our moves are awkward. We are wary, one of the other. Then, as though by divine intervention, the marionette takes on his own will, bullies me, lives beyond my own meager means. And by the enormity [*sic*] of his appetite for life begins to live me, then to write me, finally to erase me. And I wither, capably negative at last. Who directs me? Who else but my Muse, my magic marker?"

(Phew. I'll be the cynic, let someone else play simpleton. But apart from the mangling of "enormity," the passage is not ignorant. Mole has blindly pushed against a dead tree, and the rotten thing has given way to reveal a mess of busy slugs. The old Who-Pulls-My-Strings-While-I-Pull-Yours routine. Mole and I are tangled in each other's strings: I taught him, he's pointing his lessons at me. What a pair of puppets we are! We begin all curled up, sleeping, as good as dead. We discover that we can move ourselves in mysterious ways, and move others, too. Then we discover our dependence. We're controlled! We have a handler! In an act of rebellion we pull out our strings, one by one, each tug less articulate than the last. A final wrenching grope: Jubilee! Perfect freedom, all vital links cut: we fall, a jumble of sticks, nothing, mere matter.)

"Why did you write it like this, salting it with conundrums?"
"You might as well ask why I wrote it at all."
"Very well. Why did you write it at all?"
"Why won't you be polite? Why must critic and fictionist remain at war?"
"Who accused you of writing fiction?"
"You'll learn to love my book, wait and see. I love it."
"I despise it. I despise you. I despise this slop you make me eat. I'm paying for it, for Christ's sake! You might at least serve a lamb chop once in a while, or some baked ham. I'm not asking for the world, am I? I'd just now and then like to eat something other than chicken croquettes or chile or potato puffs or herring in sour cream . . ."
"Let's get back to work, Maestro, you've just used up another play period with your complaints."

"You know I'm in pain?"
"So am I."
"I wouldn't metaphor you, really, I'm in awful pain."
"Me too."
"I've got the clap."

"So do I."

"But what am I going to do about it?"

"Don't worry. Boswell had a dose most of his life, and consider what he did for Johnson."

"Mole, listen to me. Tomorrow's Independence Day. Free me, go away, let me go. Let's forget what happened here. It can come to no good end, it can come to no end at all. I've read your stuff."

"Not *stuff*, life's work."

"I've read the long work of your short life three times. I'm going to lose my wife if I don't get out my toolbox—soon—and be Mr. Fixit. I was on the brink of something when you broke in on me. I could have you boiled in piss for what you've done. Trust me, I bear you no malice, or not much. I pity you, I really do. I even blame myself for what you've become. Someday you'll be a writer, I feel it in my bones. This time I mean what I'm telling you. But it won't happen like this, by forcing things. Put away the cannon, let me go, I'll give you dough, you can fly to Costa Rica, I'll never tell a soul . . ."

"Let's get back to work. You'll get the hang of it. It's a difficult book. I'll bet it took the critics years to break the code of *Finnegans Wake*."

"But you haven't written *Finnegans Wake*. Can't I make you understand?"

"Okay, reviewer, cut the shit. Let's take it from the top again, and this time aloud."

Today he accused me of lampooning his art by reading it unmusically. I denied this vigorously. He gets tetchier by the day, and so do I. We are at stalemate.

This morning I decided to humor him a little, told him that aspects of his work were legitimately original. He applauded, clapping his hands as though we were at a canvas-back revival meeting and I were the sinner come home to dear Jesus at last. He hugged me. Then he rewarded me by authorizing me to write a full-dress critical biography of him and his work. He promises to guide me. The books—his and mine—will make us famous. I am to begin at once. "And if I refuse?" He replies at once, ready for the question: "You're as good as dead." I believe him. Stalemate is broken. I topple my king.

By and by I came to take his revolver for granted. Sometimes it seemed more like an old buddy than an instrument to write finish to Jupe. But several theatrical turns of fortune enforced on me the stubborn truth that I was his prisoner. The first had come late in June, during a play period, when we were amusing ourselves with knock-knock games.

"Knock-knock," I said.

"Who's there?" he asked.

"Isadore," I answered.

"Isadore Who?"

"Isadore Bellringing?"

He jumped up, pointed the Colt at my mouth and whispered, "Answer it, act relaxed or I'll blow away your fucking wits."

For days I brooded over his reaction to my innocent jape.

I was spooked, and decided to try an escape, worked up what I thought was an airtight plan. I waited for a night when he was more than usually weary, and when he ordered me to our bedroom (where he buried the house and car keys in the crotch of his jockey shorts and slept with his fingers cramped around the trigger guard), I proposed that I read aloud just once more a few passages from his book. He agreed, natch, to hear his words declaimed, and I read, subtly flattening my voice to a drone, and after fifty pages of metaphysics, snores rose from the land of nod. His tight grip on the Python unballed, and it fell to the floor; he didn't stir. I had him. I could leave, I could hold him under the gun till the police came, I could shoot him. I held the warm, sweat-moist piece to his temple for a while. He snored. I cocked it. He grinned in his sleep, farted. Holding the pistol against his brain-can I unzipped his fly and fished up my keys from the damp tangle where they had lain snug those many, many weeks. I would let him live. I crept from my house and threw the Colt into the dark woods. I slid behind the wheel of my Volvo and turned the key in the ignition. The starter motor churned grudgingly, but to no purpose. I searched under the hood, pulled at grease-caked wires and thumped on rusty pipes. I tapped the air cleaner. I kicked the tires. The car would not start. Presently I felt a cold blade against the back of my neck.

"You've got to know what you're doing, Maestro, before you screw around under the hood."

"What did you do to my car?" I was near tears, like a kid asking some bully why the bully has broken his bike.

"I didn't do anything. Look here. Listen." And he turned my key in the ignition of my car, which leapt alive for him and purred: *Where to? I'm ready.* The Mole and I searched for his revolver with a flashlight, and when I found it I forked it over to him.

Another time the Mole and I were playing slapjack, and rather than go for the pile of cards beneath the knave I grabbed for his pistol. He beat me to it, and then began to beat me with it, breaking my glasses.

"Now you've done it, you goddamned fool! How can I see to read? To write?"

He puzzled out a way, he always does. Obliged me to turn pages with one hand, to type with one hand, while I used a large chunk of the left lens like a monocle. The practice gave me headaches, and did nothing for my efficiency. He let me order a replacement pair from New York.

My closest call came the day that Kate telephoned for the last time. It was early August. She was enraged, bringing down curses on all my works and days. She said she was finished with me.

"Who's up there with you?"

"What do you mean, Kate?"

"What's her name? Is she one of your perky, high-titted students?"

"Please, Kate. Please?"

"You never even warned me, you filthy bastard!"

"I never warned you about what?"

Of course I knew "what." I had dreaded the moment for weeks, was exhausted by my guilt, and by my partial innocence. I was incapable of denials, apologies, fancy footwork. Would I have done better had I not been under the gun? I don't know. I know only that I can never be forgiven for the doctorly tone I used to ease her misery after she vowed that I'd "pay through the nose" for what I'd done to her: "There are remedies, Kate. It's no worse than a sore throat. I meant to warn you . . . something came up." (Would she never pick up a clue?) "Go to a doctor, it's not as bad as it seems."

"Don't you want to know how I found out that I have it? Don't you want to know, writer?"

"How did you find out?" I sighed. I missed her so gravely that while she told me I repeated her name—Kate, Kate, Kate —savoring its mint sweetness, trying to make it last. Kate. Good name, too short.

"I found out from your best friend. I gave Nick a little dose the night I returned from Seattle, and he told me, had the decency to tell me. Once more: who's up there with you?"

"There is no girl here. I'm alone. There's no human being here."

Wouldn't she check up on me, call the Brigadier, discover my lie? She wouldn't. She'd ask me. Then she'd believe me, or not believe me. I was doomed.

"Bye, Jupe."

I held the dead phone for a few seconds and heard the Mole as from afar consoling me, assuring me that I was better off without her, that people like us—*US*, for God's sake!—traveled best when we traveled light. I stared at him through my jagged bit of lens. He was wearing Kate's lumber jacket, checkerboard red and black wool. He was relaxed, composed. I was wearing a T-shirt and sweating, and I had to take a piss but I was afraid to take a piss because I knew it would hurt. What was all this? How had I come to this? Bigwit Jupe, unraveler of knots, explicator of plots, explainer, seer: see through this broken pane, explicate this design. I had been practiced upon. Then I saw it all, knew by whom I had been practiced upon. No more lag: I comprehended at last what any half-attentive detective-reader would have recognized by Chapter Seven, the identity of the outlaw's accomplice.

"Tell me about Mouse," I said.

He grinned. Then he explained how she had fingered me, set me up, knocked me off. Mole knew I'd come to Maine, but he couldn't learn where. The Mouse had telephoned him from the Brigadier's the night I left her there, the rest was elementary. I asked where she was now. He said he didn't know, didn't care. He suggested that we return to work on his life. I stood, contemplating the ruins that had been *my* life. I thought of myself corking her while my jailer pecked away at the last words of the thing that was now my cross to bear. Changing our luck: Jupe from wife to jerk, Mole from soft lead to typewriter. I realized I had read, on one of the last pages of his invention, a ribald account of a sexual encounter that the Mole had clearly cribbed from my dose-getting night. It was not fair: to be seduced, to be clapped (and probably with his vermin), to be bullied by a student, to be blocked from the execution of my life-changing work, to be set up by a quote-struck girl. I could not endure it. I hit him, fuck his pistol, should have killed him when I had the chance. A shot *rang out,* as the romancers like to write. In fact it thudded, and a bullet drilled into *The Great Gatsby*'s spine, spilling entrails of yellow pulp like dandruff on my shoulder, three inches below and to the right of the place of impact. A dreadful sound, a dreadful sight, and they brought me to my senses. I finally believed in his fanaticism, and knew he would murder me if he thought it would do his work no harm. He had no life of his own to protect. His book had obliterated him. He had no fear of death because he knew, despite the evidence, that he'd be around forever, reincarnated as three hundred pages glued to cardboard, to witness his effect on the world. He had nothing to lose: a frightening thing, an artist, the genuine article, and I was his creature.

My own work, even my poor journal, was pushed aside by the awful load of chores he obliged me to perform for him. I was made to write three, sometimes five thousand words a day. He'd read each page as he tore it from my typewriter. He might quibble with the angle I took; he'd invariably "polish," as he said, my prose. By nightfall, used up, I'd fall asleep to the beat of my machine drumming out a clean and revised draft of my high words about his low life. I didn't even know his given name, or his age. All I knew was his work. Sometimes he wrote as though he were the first man on earth, and the last. Everything under his sun was new, even the most ancient verities. His language was often overblown, like mine, and sometimes raw, but it had ardor. When I wrote the truth about what he had written he was pleased—for me. Not for himself—he had known from the beginning.

I used what little free time I had to rediscover the pleasure of reading fiction. Ran through the complete Hardy Boys— *The Tower Treasure, The Secret of the Old Mill, What Happened at Midnight,* twenty more—a book a day. And in my attic, secured by wires in bales, ready for the paper drive that never came because paper, like words, came to come so cheap, were ancient *Esquires* and *National Geographics.* The Mole would let me sit sweating under the dormers scouting up native mothers at suck and Vargas girls with creamy bigs. Pretty pleasures! The Man of Letters confessed to his authorized biographer that when he felt a man's need, he would race to his desk and let his pencil stroke blank paper. He'd dream up an erotic tale, and when it was done he would lie back and read it, fiddling with his own taut story line until he had brought himself off. Write, read, whip! Welcome to Parnassus! He fell into his habit when he realized that sweet-talking the girls, undressing them, doing them, lingering post-coitus for small talk—all the unzipping and unbuckling and noise-making— was a useless expense of time. So he gave it up almost entirely, and cooked up his self-serving rigmarole. With the full approval of his better half: his Muse, my Mouse.

We slept together, at his insistence, in the canopied four-poster where Kate and I used to sleep. He liked me close, the better to keep tabs on me, the better to pump me on matters of craft and the tricks of publication. It was my lot in the dead of night to map his publicity campaign, to debate the merits of publication dates. (Was May better than November? Was his book better fit for a Christmas present or a beach-blanket read?) Finally, to anticipate his wordly questions before he asked them, and to vacate myself of replies, I put together the kind of *Q & A* booklet orthodontists give the parents of kids about to get braces:

Q: Are braces uncomfortable?
A: They needn't be, if a qualified orthodontist . . .
Q: Are braces expensive . . .
A: This depends on your definition of *expensive.* Some people . . .
Q: Will anyone review my book?
A: This depends on your definition of *review.*

I titled this booklet *When Your Novel Is Published: A Guide to Marboro Country.*

*   *   *

One day, to reward me for an energetic run of work that required little revision, he announced that he was going to town to buy me a present. He locked me in the bathroom to prevent my escape, and—incredibly—I found myself missing him. When he returned an hour later he brought penicillin. A few days later I was cured. He didn't use the medicine. He suffered, if he suffered, in silence.

A Western Union man slipped a telegram under my door, and stole away. Didn't want to bother the reclusive artist. Marked on its envelope: *deliver by hand—prepaid reply requested.* From Kate: LIED ABOUT NICK STOP IT HASN'T HAPPENED YET STOP COME HOME PLEASE STOP STOP STOP STOP

Finally I noticed the pistol was missing. I realized then that I hadn't seen it for days. There was no further need for it. Our collaboration was almost at its end, the summer was almost gone. Nothing could have made me break off work on my book about him. An unfinished book almost finished compels its imperatives more remorselessly than any shooting iron.

The Master and the Muse[1]

"Once upon a time my master promised me that I was different from the others, and better, and that a novel was my destiny, and he spoke true, and I gave my life to the writing of it."

Thus, in his stiff-collared words, begins the curious history of a Man of Letters, a young man, inhabited by demons, whose life it has been my own lesser destiny to retail. A critic surrenders himself to the contemplation of creators, but too seldom is

[1]This variant text of my title chapter is one of several that my publisher rejected. It's my favorite. When Mole and I discussed it we followed the vulgar but common practice of calling it by an abbreviated title: he knew it as *Master*, I called it *Muse*, my publisher belittled it with the moniker *M'n'M*.

he privileged to discover an artist worthy of his self-sacrifice. To unearth such a one as this imposes on the biographer a lifelong responsibility, but provides him with a lifelong raison d'être. I mean to say that I owe the world this remarkable man's story.

I first met him many years ago. He was my student then, as I am now his. He called me maestro, with affection rather than irony. When he left my care I sent him into the world with the modest investment of my advice, sat back, and waited for the returns to roll in.[2] But listen while he, for the moment, picks up the spoor of his first poor days as a fictioneer:

"I had some money, very little. I supplemented the pissant fellowship the University had given me by selling textbooks I stole from the Student Union while the kids wasted their afternoons drinking pop and swapping carnal lies. I'd take their books—a Gladstone bag at a swipe—and haul them downtown to Barnes & Noble, and fence them at the used-book counter. That's where I learned the transitory value of nonfiction. Textbook prices fell into black holes, you wouldn't believe it! A 12th edition always elbowed aside the 11th, and today's Nobel Laureate in microbiology was tomorrow's out-of-print fool. (Had I known that novels, which on principle I wouldn't steal, couldn't have been fenced at any price, were in plain words worthless, I would have been shaken, but not deflected from my course.)

---

[2]The attentive reader will sense, as well as know, that this account is frequently at variance with the facts. Need I remark that it enhances the Mole considerably, and at my expense? There was some give-and-take here: he gave me the sentence about "maestro" (hedging it about, perhaps, with irony) and I gave him all the rest, the preposterous statement that there had been imposed on me a "lifelong responsibility." I didn't believe that when I wrote it, and I guess I don't believe it now. I gave more than I got, for sure. Okay, don't lose sight of the gun.

"Times were hard then. But I reckoned I could hang tight for nine months. By then I'd produce a masterwork, or kill myself. But how to proceed? So many hurdles, so many. The highest was friendlessness. Because I had no buddies, it followed that I had no pull, no publishing crony to tip me to the hot, easy-to-boost subjects, no one to turn a key in a locked door. My low hurdles were three: plot, character, purpose. I knew no story that I wanted to tell. I needed inhabitants for my nonexistent scenes, and all I could dream up were runny noses, damp eyes, and speechless mouths. I had no notion who my men and women were, or why they should be. Once upon a time they had come to life merely because they were due at a creative-writing class. Now I knew only that I had to become a writer because I had to become a writer. To stiffen my creative dick I dreamt of myself as Robert Frost talking to an interviewer, looking back across the years at his purpose, making with his liver-spotted fingers and hands a steepled chapel, saying: *There's room for only one person at a time. I always meant that person to be me.* Amen."

For the Man of Letters it was a time in the desert, a season of doubt and self-abasement. Then, finally, he heard The Call. He had been wandering Morningside Heights, his head empty, when he listlessly broke for lunch. He found his way by chance to a tavern and ordered apple juice and chile. No sooner had he spooned his bowl clean than a mighty commotion commenced in his interior territories. Something of power had taken hold of him, was shaking his depths. The chile! He pinched shut his sphincter and lunged at the door marked *Caballeros.* Home free, he sat with his britches around his pipestem ankles, thundering and gushing when—suddenly— he felt a flash, heard voices, and his novel came to him, courtesy of Señorita Providencia y Suerte. It rushed at him loaded with options, plotted and peopled from prologue to afterword.

What to do? He couldn't hazard losing this gift from the Muse. So while he sat voiding his turbulent belly he jotted, on sheets of glossy tan bung-wipe, the outline of the immortal effluvia blown his way by a vagrant wind. Impatient customers banged on the door. "Wait," he begged, "I'm not done," and he simulated the roars and groans of expulsion. Soon the barman joined the ugly mob outside the Mole's serendipitous study, and threatened to "have [his] ass." But the Man of Letters worked away, filling the tiny sheets with notes and boss words and character sketches sufficient to conceive a thriving youngling of imaginary prose. When he had covered the last of the paper with his improvised shorthand, he turned to the lavatory walls and Magic-Markered his aesthetic design among fond boasts, illegible riddles and indecent invitations. Finished finally, exhausted by his labors *in contrapunto,* he came forth. Three roughnecks stood by the door and of course they would say *Phew, wotta stink, sumpn muster died inair.* The Man of Letters could only grin tolerantly at their artless calumnies. He left, cocksure in the conviction that writ on the toilet paper bunched in his pocket was half of a first-class ticket to immortality. The other half was securely hidden among the sentiments and likenesses on the shithouse walls.

He rushed home, eager to find his way to the substance of his finally realized essence. His room was a ten-foot-square cell in a derelict tenement that the university had bought for the use of the Creative Arts Program as a rehearsal hall. He paid flophouse prices for the room, a buck a day. There was neither heat nor plumbing, and he was not meant to live in it overnight, but rules had been stretched. What painful events followed his return there he reluctantly narrated to me:

"I sat overlooking an air shaft at a table that held my hot plate and books and writing gear, and prepared to begin. In the rehearsal room to my left some guy with a Chinese accent was warbling "Bill" from *Showboat.* He couldn't find the key. He kept trying. I had to bang against my wall to shut him up. I spread my toilet paper in front of me and tried to read my excited script. Sentences snaked all over the place, crossing one another, sometimes running right off the edges of the paper, which was now soggy from sweat. The ink was beginning to blot. I studied my outline, held it up to my gooseneck lamp, turned it this way and that way. Blinked at it. No use. Not a word or a character of what I had scribbled in such haste and exultation could I read. I sat through the hot night hitting my forehead with my palm, praying for some illumination. My God, even a recollection would do! By sunup I felt my belly rumble. I limped slump-shouldered down the hall to the can, and used for their principal purpose the stern-sheets that had once held my hopes, while I wept on the tile floor, cold beneath my thin-soled shoes.

"But wait! The other half: I had forgotten it! I hoisted my pants and raced through the gray morning streets to the tavern, and waited in its doorway till opening time. A few hours later the sullen barkeep arrived to clean up, and as soon as the door was off its lock I barged past him, ignoring his sarcasms: *Hi, pooper, can I bring you something to read in there, some pretty pictures to look at? Or did you come to take a nap?* I opened *Caballeros,* and switched on the light. The overhead fan began to sing. And there, before my befuddled and horrified eyes, four clean walls, not a trace left behind, not of pornographic sketches, or assignations, or limericks, or of the working outline for the most praiseworthy fiction to be made since the death of James Joyce. In place of yesterday's inspiration I found a blackboard, with chalk and eraser and instructions—GENTS: WRITE HERE, BE NICE. I ran to the bar and bearded the oaf polishing glasses: *Who stole my novel? Who ripped off my best stuff?* He put aside his towel and reached for a pool cue, and I stumbled out the door into the insulting light. My game was up.

"I was desolate. Where was justice? Then I fell into a rage, and promised myself that somebody would by God pay for what I had suffered. I crossed busy streets against red lights, shaking my fist at the drivers who yelled abuse at me as they swerved to avoid me. I wanted them to hit me, to run me down so that they would be ruined in court when my survivors sued their asses off. Wait a minute! What survivors? I had no family, no one who cared a fiddler's fuck about me.

"So I decided to find you. You had set it all moving. I could thank you for my aches and bruises. You had promised me I was a comer, a bona-fide wonderboy. I blamed you for the hours and days and weeks I had wasted making lapidary studies of the British nobility doing intrigues in Venice. I blamed you for the squalor I called home. I was a thief, thanks to you. My head pounded all the time, thanks to you. I wanted to track you down and ask you some hard questions, and if you flunked my quiz . . . I was ready for anything."

But he didn't find me.

Not that summer.

Finally he circled back to his miserable cell to begin another novel. He was to begin dozens, to try hundreds of false beginnings. And while he sat at his makeshift desk, his eyes burning from sweat and salt tears, trying to make something of himself, trying to re-create himself by jumping from his own soiled skin into the hide of James or Faulkner or Hemingway, his inventive centers were dead to the juicy life everywhere around him.

Every day he would pass in the halls of his tenement the creative ragtag that abounded just beyond his field of vision. There was the son of a steel magnate, a would-be Willy Loman. There was the cheerful coed dying to be Ophelia, whose wooden leg received serial coats of stain so that it turned a deeper tan after each weekend of good beach weather. Sopranos ran their arias, and soprano saxophonists wailed. New-minted artists climbed the stairs to studios carrying the painter's kit—easel, palette, smock, and beret—that was sold as a loss leader in the University Store. Artists' models passed him wearing only bathrobes, and he never noticed. His mind's eye was on Snopes country or the diamond as big as the Ritz or Kilimanjaro—places he'd never been, places he'd never go.

It was at this depression in his career that the Man of Letters met his Muse. The day was busy with heat lightning and thunder. He was sitting, as usual, at his desk, failing, as usual, at beginnings. She knocked on his open door, asked herself in to rest her dogs. She was a model, and she was naked beneath a worn terry-cloth robe. She was beautiful; he tumbled into love.

Whoa up, my readers will protest, *not so fast!* Love is no such hit-and-runner, you believe. Love is a sneak thief, a wheedling Bible salesman of the emotions, winning the customer over the hard way, by inches. Only in fictional romances can love for girl follow discovery of girl by only a single predicate and subject: we are meant to be dealing here in biography, not in bedtime stories.

Quite so. But you must understand that my subject, dwelling utterly in fiction's inky realm, reacted precisely like a hero of fiction's devious and compressed design. He saw, he articulated, he loved. She, too, was steeped in artifice, simulated emotion, metaphor, fortuitous juxtaposition, art.

He invited her into his room, and she sat cross-legged on his unmade bed, sighing that she was whipped half to death, complaining that she'd had to pose all morning.

"What's it like?" he asked.

"The fine arts have been a disappointment to me. I thought I could bathe in the painter's reflected glory, so to speak. I want to cause something beautiful. But they never make anything much of me. Maybe I'm not beautiful enough to inspire anything that's beautiful."

"Oh no, not at all, I think you're the most beautiful thing I've ever seen."

She neither agreed with this judgment nor disputed it. She began instead to read aloud from a book she had brought with her, and was immediately absorbed by it. (As chance would have it, the book was by Yrs. Trly., a thing called *Another, Better World*, my first cry, as eager an act of tub-thumping for the whimsies of imagination as adolescent fervor could conceive. The Man of Letters has *assured* me that she was indeed, at that critical moment, reading me. A coincidence, to be certain, but one I will accept on faith.[3])

"Hey!" he cried out. "I know the author! He's my teacher, or he was. Quite a man, a real wizard."

They fell at once to lively talk about the merits of my work, and she pumped him for information about me: Was I mar-

[3]Once, riding the subway, I stood above a man reading with meticulous attention his *New York Times*, page upon page, ignoring the story-jumps. He came to a review of my book—a later book than *Another, Better World*—and read a line or two, examined a photograph of me, looked up at me. My heart leapt. He shut his *Times*, folded it, and closed his eyes, and let the rattling train rock him to sleep. Something died, as they say, in me.

ried? To whom? Was I *cute?* Was I this, was I that? The Man of Letters, with characteristic candor, has confessed to me that he laid on our friendship a bit thick, suggesting without actually saying so that we were *tight,* that he was privy to my prejudices and fears, and to deeper confidences he could not betray. She nodded and gee-whizzed. They had hooked each other.

The Mole has described her elsewhere: eyes set deep in a noble brow, lips stained with ink from a fountain pen whose nib she tasted with her tongue tip, a quick snake's tongue testing the sweetness of a flower between frequent underscorings of my instructions and speculations. Her fingers also were stained, and from the pocket of her robe peeked a bouquet of colored paper strips from which she picked bookmarks to set apart for agreement or disputation some passage of mine that had particularly arrested her.

I can imagine the effect on him of her long white neck, and her breasts—small and plump, high and cheerful, a bit cross-eyed, negligently covered by the soft terry-cloth—and her bare feet, dirty from the unswept floor and with their toenails painted orange. Her legs, gangly and pale, must have made a fine sight curled carelessly under her bare and perfect ass while the thunder bumped the world and lightning shot and the Mole sweated and itched. Were he an ordinary kind of creature, he would have looked her over and realized at once that she was so far beyond and above his rough manners, his (let me be candid) undistinguished physiognomy, his underachievements, that merely to address her was to venture an impudence. But he was as ignorant of his inconsequence as any man could be. He saw only a reader, a gorgeous reader reading by destiny's direction the right book, the only book for that moment.

So they name-dropped authors and traded the gossip other-wise called The Wisdom of the Ancients. She seemed to admire whomsoever she had read.

"Oh, he's *great*" (can I not hear her?) "and his novel, too, simply great!"

Every title he mentioned, she knew. The close community of their enthusiasms astounded them, and when she was finally called back to the studio by an instructor *(C'mon, honey, time to show your stuff)*, it was with the understanding that they would meet again.

And so they did. They met day after day, and every day he gave her a book. At first he stole these gifts from the Student Union, but soon, as he began to appreciate the sophistication of her needs, he raided further afield: Brentano's, Scribner's, the Strand, the Gotham Book Mart. He yielded his principle, his injunction against boosting novels: what could he do? She liked them. Finally he was obliged in his search for novelty to wear his heavy, amply pocketed trench coat into the deepest, hottest innards of specialty book dealers. As long as he held the line at American or English writers, or Europeans in translation, as long as he dealt in poetry, aesthetics, and fiction—especially fiction—he never once caught her with her ignorance showing. Of all things else beneath the sun she was unknowing and uncaring. Just like him.

Weeks passed, and still he hid his trump up his sleeve. He permitted her to talk to him as though they were equals, a couple of fans, constant readers, monk and nun forsaking all else to love Gutenberg. Finally her enthusiasm for a chunk of Poe's juvenilia moved her to squeal in delight, to touch his thigh, and he played his wild card.

"I'm a writer, too, you know. I'm a . . . novelist."

As easy as that: blackjack, the bank was bust. She didn't invite him to make love to her at once. Some reserve of cunning had survived her intemperate enthusiasms, and she asked what he was writing, and whether it was "in fact" finished, and whether it "in fact" had a publisher. But before he could stammer an evasion, she dismissed her own questions.

"Don't talk about your work," she admonished him, "not even to me. Talk has been the ruin of many a writer."

She did ask to see a sample, not at his place but at hers, and the quid for the quo was understood. He promised to bring her a "nice chunk" next day, and she left to show God knew what to God knew whom. His heart was swollen; so, too, his vital gristle. He was frantic to begin. He cleared his desk, angled his pencil and headed his first chapter. He felt himself poised on the edge of a breakthrough. He felt himself. Was it possible that his inspiration of the month before, lost to sewers and the sea, was creeping up on him again? Was lightning prepared to strike twice the same desperate aspirant? Characters began to assume shimmering form, like the phantom outlines of a photographic print when it's first dipped in the juice. Flesh began to stick to bones, a third dimension was just yonder, beckoning. He felt exalted. But his pencil angled lower and lower. A few raspy scratches against the paper and it flopped over stricken, impotent.

"I even prayed. But nothing helped. I hid from her a couple of days. She taped a note against my door: *Where's the ms? I'm waiting. A deadline is a deadline.* I was beside myself, would write anything, let any words do, I'd worry later about immortality. Nothing, still nothing. Next day, another note: *Bring the ms. tomorrow or forget me, and I'll forget you. I hate non-writing writers.* I considered suicide. I even considered plagiarism, but I knew it would never work; she had read everything I liked enough to claim as my own.

"Finally I was reduced to showing her my kid stuff, my Creative Writing stories. Just like I was some undergraduate wooing his mixer date with a ham-handed improvisation of the final graphs of "The Dead." I sat watching her read. My muscles were slack, I felt ashamed. She bent over the pages, squinting. She shook her head once, lifted her eyebrows. Finally she turned the last page and grinned. I stiffened. *I'll take you, you'll do.* Thus I won her, and made her mine for good, and tricked her into believing I would be hers. Poor dear."

7

As we drove toward the finish line, toward Labor Day and an
end to my labor, we enjoyed what long-distance runners call the
kick, a fit of speed, indifference to pain. We worked dawn to
dawn getting his story down. I'd take his testimony, write it,
he'd amend my draft and type a fair copy while I grabbed an
hour's sleep. He seemed never to rest. Why the rush I couldn't
have guessed, but I took it on faith that we were working
against a deadline.

He was forthcoming about his lash-up with the Mouse. It
was a match made atop Helicon, the writer's peg slap in the
reader's hole. Weeks passed, and he rode the crest, whipped
to work by her luscious carnality. She paid him with her pussy,
the bill was a thousand words a bang; make up, make out.
Trouble was, the words weren't worth much, so the Mouse got
screwed both ways. He'd been working the vein of the rehearsal

hall, knocking together a fictional vaudeville routine, but he couldn't get the rehearsers' voices right. If only he'd listened! After a couple of weeks the lode ran out. They agreed then to forswear sex, on the theory that she was stealing his time and he was wasting his creative juices. To no avail celibacy: if he no longer came, neither did his words. The partners fell into lethargy and silence; the taste of literary discourse had gone sour in their mouths.

Now the Mouse had no employment after she gave up posing for painters and sculptors. Her Man of Letters nagged at her to infiltrate the enemy, to get a job—any would do— in the publishing game, to bring back editorial how-to and what-to from behind the lines. This she refused to do: she would not profane her word-worship by sitting 9 to 5 on Mammon's lap. She instead spent her days in the reading room of the Public Library. The Mole, indifferent as he was to the world's sweets and spangles, couldn't fail to notice that he was eating irregularly, that the electricity and water had been shut off, that Something Must Be Done.

The Mouse took to the streets. Because her beauty stopped hearts, the streets she walked were shade-treed Upper East Siders that connect Madison with Park, Park with Lexington. She'd pick up a decent-looking, literate-looking fellow and turn a single trick a night for fifty dollars. The work was easy, the money was nice, and as artist and artist's moll they were above such workaday inhibitions as jealousy or remorse. They would have done okay, would have made out, were it not for the implacable blankness of the foolscap of the Man of Letters. He told me, off the record, how it was:

"I was dry. I had wasted so much time pondering questions about voice and point of view and authorial dependability and all the rest of the arcane impedimenta you had unloaded on me that I had lost my capacity to hunt humans, to comprehend their customs or even hear and see them. I needed people, and their stories. I had words, but no one to utter them. I could create technical narrative problems, and sometimes even overcome them. So what?

"I finally realized that I'd have to kidnap life off the streets and get it to my desk if I was ever going to grab a feel off posterity. I wanted to create a compendium, a book of all generations and classes and geographies. I wanted something as comprehensive as the census and as well-wrought as a sestina." He looked at me archly. "I think you'll agree that I've made that book?" I nodded, shook my head, nodded. "We had all the trade the Mouse could want. We might have had a quiet, decent life together . . .

"But that wasn't how it was. Instead I had a Big Idea. You might say that my Big Idea is father to these pages you've learned to respect and to love. Anyway, the Mouse and I had sometimes talked about having her branch out a bit, turning her into a regular hooker for a while till we had put enough by so I could retire to Mexico or Europe for a couple of years. It was her idea, but I discouraged it. We looked out for each other, it wasn't all Number One with me, I didn't want her to sacrifice her reading time on my account. Then, bingo! The unriddling of many dilemmas in a single swipe. The Mouse began working bars, moving fast, no coy stuff. She'd spin a few times on her stool, take a bite from a peach—buzz, the bee flew to the flower. We had only one rule in this game: she took what came, no special come-ons for the appetizing numbers, no rejection slips for the dogs. She'd haul our John back to the apartment, turn a trick for twenty bucks—and give better than she got, as you damned sure know—and then stun the bejesus out of him. 'Look,' she'd ask, 'how'd you like for me to give you back ten bucks?' The deal was sweet: she'd refund half her fee, plus give a little something in trade, if the guy would tell his life's story. The whole history, half an hour's worth, his favorite food, maybe a dream or two, his pet peeve, the worst thing he'd ever done, the most unjust punishment he'd ever suffered, what he'd do with a million. They always agreed. New England boarding school headmasters, Southern sheriffs, preachers, housewives, novelists, editors, agents, even a reviewer. She'd lie naked on top of the bed scribbling shorthand about the time a skunk got into this one's tent at summer camp, or how that one got so lonely boozing without friends that he turned his neighbor's mutt into an alcoholic—*Come on, Prince, let's pop open another couple of frosties, what do you say?* Meantime the taleteller would keep his hands busy while he talked, the way Americans like to. We were raking in money, I got all the material I could ever use, and more, tons of stuff, what you've read. One day I had done almost all that was to be done. So I hauled my Muse in off the street, and fucked her day and night for a week, and then I sent her out to turn one final trick . . ."

Your master: me. We fished the same polluted pond. What now?

"Now? It's publish or perish, just like you always used to say."

Labor Day. My self-regard, my powers of discrimination, perhaps my wife and probably my novel: I had lost them all.

"Don't fret," he soothed. "You've always had me, and you'll always have me."

His promise was a threat I tried to ignore. "What now?" I asked him, in the voice of an analyst asking his client a valedictory question—*Is there anything else you wish to discuss?*—

even as he rings for the next complainer to be sent in.

"There is," the Mole confessed, "one final question. Is it publishable?"

I left him hanging for a few seconds. Imagine me pulling at my brier, had I a brier, and squinting at the truth painted on my ceiling in characters only I could read, and sighing. Petty revenge, that sigh. I forced myself to speak.

"Well, yes. Yes, it may be publishable. Not now, of course, not yet. It needs work, years of work. But you're young, and persistent—shoo, persistent is no word for what you are. And you have the loyalty of a beautiful woman."

"Will my book live forever?"

"What a question! Who asks such questions? What's *forever*, these days? A year? Four months?"

"I mean will it be a classic?"

"You're a classic, I'll tell you that."

He slipped past my irony easily enough, irony turned against that Mole stung like squirts from a leaky hose, my shots had no muzzle velocity, never raised a welt. He sized me up. He was considering me for a job. Maybe yes, maybe no. The application looked fine, the interview had not been so success-ful, and now the recommendations were coming on too iffy. No, sorry, he thought not.

"Okay, I'll let you do it. I want you to prepare my manu-script for publication. You can type it, file down the rough edges, sweeten it with bits and pieces of whatever wisdom your years have brought you. I trust you not to screw up my work. What higher honor could I pay you? Are you proud?"

He had astonished me into gentleness. "I can't do it, son. I can't think for you, or judge which words to spare and which to execute. I don't write like you. Maybe you write a little like me, but that's different, we're different, we're not fused.

Maybe I'm better than you, maybe I'm even worse, I don't know. You shouldn't have asked me. I'm about to begin my own life as an imaginative writer; it's late in the afternoon for me. You've taught me some things, true, but you've also cost me . . . cost me . . . everything . . . almost everything."

"Jupe." He had never called me that before, and I winced to hear in his mouth the word I had last heard Kate speak. "Jupe, let me level with you: you're the best critic alive, you know my work better than anyone, I've seen to that. You've been more than just a teacher to me, you've been my *primum mobile* as you might say, do I pronounce it correctly? For all these reasons you're well fixed to complete what I've begun. I'm not promising it will be easy. Quote: *Who ever promised that what endures is easily won?* Close quote, Jupe. It may take years, but you've got years of life left. Right?" I nodded, eager to agree with that hindmost declarative sentence. "Okay. Now, as for your own work, your so-called fiction: I read it one night while you were sleeping, forgive me, I had my reasons, curiosity, whatever. I'll tell you the truth: your stuff eats it. It's arch, self-conscious, two-for-a-penny, smart-ass and ironical. It doesn't shock, it isn't comely, and it isn't even true, if you know what I mean by true. You're no creative writer. I'm doing you a favor to tell you this, believe me. Hitch your wagon to my star and you'll be famous someday. What do you say?"

"I say fuck yourself."

"That's not a critic's considered response, it's unworthy of you."

"Fuck your work. That's a critic's considered response. Both it and you are botched fabrications. That's a critic's considered judgment."

"You didn't write that in your critical biography." He

tapped the mountain of manuscript that had risen between us from the surface of my worktable.

"But you don't believe I believe that junk, you ignorant mess. I don't. It was your gun, only your gun, that made me apostrophize your *noble march of nouns,* your *awful penetrations,* your etceteras. Do you comprehend the motive for my favor? Not your words, your firearm!"

"Here it is, the good old black-and-white." He again tapped the pages.

"But I'll disavow it all. The first cop I find, I'll turn you in. You'll burn. I'll withdraw every word I wrote about you."

"No you won't. I've thought it through. You won't repudiate my genius." He slipped into his gloves. Reached into his backpack and drew the thing out. Loaded. Cocked. I understood.

"You're going to shoot me, then use what I wrote to get yourself in print. Jesus, you'll murder me to get yourself published."

"*Murder* you?" He frowned, as though thinking the matter through. Then he grinned. "Oh no, nothing like that. No such thing as that. How can you think it? You've been good to me. You gave me my first shove. You've given me free room and grub all summer, and I appreciate it. You've written a peach of a book about me. You won't deny what you've written because you've written the truth, and you're a sucker for the truth. I didn't elect you casually. Now you're tired, and perhaps a little cross with me for having told you what's what with your fiction, the little of it I read. I understand. But now you're going to help some more, prepare my script for publication, find it a good home, someone worthy of it. You'll tend to the odds and ends, do the monkey work . . ."

"You'd better shoot, pal. Because if you don't I'll see you dead, snuff you myself . . ."

"There you are, Maestro, the high cost of making beautiful things, Q.E.D."

"High cost, my ass! A sore butt, maybe. Perhaps a paper cut—"

"You still don't comprehend, Professor. It's so painful, solitary, celibate—"

"Oh my sweet Christ! Behold your servant Mole. Celibate! With his firecracker's wick smoldering, the works set to explode, sparked by rubbing his own defiled stub. Celibate! A writer, already, a pimp!"

And at that instant, pat and bang on cue, she materialized. Standing in the same doorway where I had discovered him thirteen weeks ago, thirteen hundred millennia ago. Herself, blank as a page, a mattressback for Art.

"Hi, you guys! Almost finished, honey? You said to come Labor Day, and here I am." Then, sensing that she owed more respect to her elder, she addressed me with counterfeit gravity: "Isn't he great, sir? Isn't he a great novelist? Don't you love him? Won't you find him a publisher?"

The Man of Letters didn't speak to her. Instead he commanded her with his revolver to sit beside me, and she complied, still grinning with excitement.

He spoke to me: "Hate me if you want, you always have, I know that."

"I told you that, son."

"Please yourself. Once, when I was alone in the world, I cared what you and your frat-house students thought about me. It doesn't matter anymore, I've got my work, and you don't hate *it*, no matter what you say now. That's why I'll leave my book in your trust, you'll care for it as though it's your own. In a way it is yours, at least in part. We're in it together. I'm the poet, you're the mechanic. I make, you fix. If you need money, she'll get it for you, she knows how."

She was puzzled, wounded. "What are you saying, honey?" She whined, her lower lip trembled, she was just a groupie, no Muse at all, just a pushover named Mouse, a minus digit in the complicated score we'd been keeping.

The Mole ignored her. He fiddled with the Colt Python, stared into its tight, greasy hole, and then I saw it all, saw by flash his last act illumined, saw the epilogue, the end of me.

"Don't do it, son. You're a special case, they broke the mold . . . Save yourself for other books. Better books . . . Wait: this one is . . . fine, the thing itself."

"Do you mean that?"

" . . . . "

"Answer me."

"I guess."

"Answer. Yes or no?"

"Yes."

Happy days. He grinned, laid down the revolver. "Then you'll do it, beat it into shape for me? Get it in print?"

"Yes," I sighed, surrendering.

"Word of honor?"

"Word of honor."

"I knew you'd do it. You'd never let them ignore me, my baby. But you need help, some of the old whizzbang P/R to light up the star. And I'm going to give it to you. I'm going to shove this black snake in my mouth, and let it kiss me, a soul kiss . . ."

She was begging him, babbling endearments, telling him

how good he was, what a great lover, what a great writer, how much better he was than the rest of us, how much better than me, as a lover, as a writer . . .

"Shut up! I know all that! Of course my life is more valuable than his, just as his is more valuable than yours. Don't you think I know that? You were put on earth to clean up my office, like he was put here to clean up my prose. You're here to shill for me and fuck me and feed me. Count yourselves lucky to have been my creatures. Not an uninteresting couple of characters, let your author give you your due. I'd happily drill you both, if it would serve my purpose. It doesn't. As it happens, I'm done with writing. I'll settle for what I've made. It's enough, more than enough . . ."

"You inkling! Lower case! Semicolon! WRITER! Pull that fucking trigger, artist, pull it. Don't pull it! Stop! I didn't mean what I said . . ."

Part Three
CLEANING UP

It all ended two years ago, ephemeron by the measure of literary history, eternity for me. There was no trial, just a coroner's inquest. Because the police found the Mouse huddled sobbing in the back seat of my Volvo there was some suspicion of foul play in the Bangor and Bar Harbor papers, some gossip that I had killed him fighting for the girl. Science saved this old humanist's ass, the science of death by gunshot, the science of bullet vectors and blood types, microscopic analysis of the bits of brain and fluid—as milky as semen—that they picked out of my hair. Still, many believe to this day that I drove him to shoot himself. He was so sensitive, they say, I'm so tough. The D.A. from the county seat presumed he must have been suffering some terminal illness (aren't we all?), and this forced his hand. He ordered an autopsy, but I could have saved the taxpayers some money if the D.A. had listened to me:

the Medical Examiner gave the Mole a clean bill of health, just as I predicted. He was fit as a mongrel dog, didn't even have the clap, he'd hornswoggled me on that, too.

No kinsman claimed his body. He left a Last Will and Testament, all very correct, properly witnessed and notarized. Named me his literary executor, with the encouraging footnote that he had produced sufficient words to "last my master a lifetime." No vigorish, though, no cut for the dealer. I spent a year pulling together his loose ends, and a lot of good it's done me. Shoo, he was shrewd. The publicity after his death, and no work of mine, brought six bids for his book at auction. I controlled the rights, even though the cunning bastard had assigned me no profit from them, and I held a gun to the publisher's head and insisted we go out as an entry, his novel —*Kisses and Tales*—and my critical biography—*The Master and the Muse*. Blood splashed him into fame. He did what my crapshooting chums called making the point the hard way, but I guess he got it made. When I insisted that our books be published in matching editions, bound in blue and boxed, the publisher balked at the box, and soon enough I learned why. The treacherous shysters printed ten times as many copies of the Mole's thing as they did of mine, and they went back to press for him twice before publication date. For me? Never. A single bitty printing, and that's all she wrote. Some matching editions! His was as solid as a dictionary, bound with sturdy boards and covered with royal blue cloth as rich as velvet. Did they think I had no eyes to see the mess they made of *The Master and the Muse*? Did they think I wouldn't notice, or be wounded, by the temporary thing it is? I have eyes to see the banal dust jacket, I can see the uneven line of type on the spine and title page, I can feel the pulpy paper, I know only too well that the ink stains your fingers, that the violent taking-off of

the Man of Letters thrust me into the shadows, that the bul-
lyboy roughhouse of his story overwhelms my telling of it. I
know all this. I'm not blind, after all, though sometimes I wish
I were, and invisible too. I'm still a critic, of sorts. I do know,
sometimes, what's what, what will endure and what will not.
Take me, for instance, inching through life but still on the case.

Most of the reviews of *Kisses and Tales* were gee-whizzers.
The Mole is outclassing Marvels at Clapper's this season, and
Marvels just brought home his first NBA, so much for prophecy. The reviews of *M'n'M* rankled, no kidding. The word was
out, the fix was in, they had me fingered for oblivion. I can't
even now bear to discuss what most of them said about my
book, about me. Scharmon wrote an interminable notice for
the *NYRB* and killed my biography—the prick—with kind-
ness. He praised its "sturdy fidelity to fact, its scrupulous regard
for chronologies"; he appreciated its "refusal to stoop to gossip
or exploit the spectacular," gave full marks to its "quiet decorum" and "Swiss efficiency. What matter if the book is dull?"
the assassin asked my potential readers. "Let more creative
interpreters have their later say. Here are the archives."

I'm on my ass, of course, wide to the sky. If bad reviews hurt
the *Master*, indifferent reviews and no reviews hurt it worse.
Shoo, when Baby Hughie interviewed me he never even mentioned my book or its title, he just pumped me for gory spe-
cifics, for "color." Which made it painful for me to borrow
money from him to buy an ad for my story of the Mole. I know,
but what the hell: if the publishers won't support what they're
trying to peddle, somebody has to. I plucked some nouns and
adjectives from Scharmon: "FACT: SPECTACULAR GOS-
SIP! . . . CREATIVE!!!!" They didn't help, nothing helps,
who reads books these days, who reads ads?

What a killer! Here are the archives! Irony is that *The*

Master and the Muse is shot through with half-truths, omissions and special pleadings. I begged my readers to forgive my Man of Letters his petty burglaries, his felonies, his extortions, his pimpery. My few readers were happy to forgive the miscreant his crimes, to regard him as a latter-day St. Genet, but safe in the boneyard where he couldn't get at decent folks' daughters or silver. Why did I plead for a light sentence for him? I don't know. He *was* quite a writer, and there's my investment in him . . .

His royalties were earmarked for a fund for struggling you-know-whats. I've already made two awards in the amount of the annual interest from his fruitful estate. I gave one to a poet for the editorial page of a small-town weekly. She is highly prized by its readers, especially during the autumn months when she versifies of loss, betrayal and apple cider. The other grant I gave to Nick—*no hard feelings* was to have been the theme of my generosity, forgiveness through and through. I didn't care whether I ever set eyes on him again, but I would welcome another book from him. And perhaps a small kickback, these things I thought were understood. So far no token from him, and he doesn't answer his telephone. Listen, I could use the money: I lost my job at the university, they hated to let me go, they said, but Fugelman's complaints, the unresolved subplots, the publicity—*you understand?*—their hands were tied, they said.

My dreams come to me mostly in the medium of reviews and essays, Latinate prose, no pix. In fact my review assignments fell off steeply from the very beginning of my life post-Mole. I couldn't think what to think anymore, and I began to wish to please more than to judge, and I watched my pieces drift further and further toward the back of the bus, from page three to page eight, to the middle of the *Times*. Finally, there

I was, in the high thirties, slumming with the AMAZE YOUR FRIENDS!! ads, and the jig was up.

It hasn't been easy. Kate took me back for a few weeks, but she could no longer live at ease with me. So she said. Even when she learned the truth. The truth, she said, was bad enough. While I was under the Mole's gun she told me she didn't care what I said, that she could respond only to what I did. Later she changed her tune, said she couldn't drive out my cold words. Words stuck, she said, they counted. I guess I understand. I should. And it's true enough, as she says, that the Mouse held no gun to my sensual regions the night I betrayed my wife and myself.

Nick courts Kate. He gave up his dancer that catastrophic summer. No one's satisfied with what he has. I guess I understand. I should. He's doing better now, I hear. The novel looms. He's okay, a good man. Robin likes him. They go to Knick games together. I don't resent my old friend. Not much. But Kate will never settle for him. (It can't be possible to have killed her love by the things I said, and didn't say, against my will. Can it? Can't any words be erased?)

I moved in with the Mouse for a week, no monkey business, take my word. She wasn't much interested in me, but I needed her for research. Saw her again last year. She hadn't lost her looks, but she wasn't any fun either. Her heart went quite out of literature after seeing close up a wet, noisy final chapter. Some bits and pieces of the Man of Letters got caught in her hair, too, and she didn't like it. When it happened I saw the muse-ship leak out of her quite as quickly as the fancy and ambition leaked out of him, and now she works for a company that makes paper shredders, and all that's left of the old style is an occasional *Oh wow* or *Jeez*, and she remembers him with a shake of her head: *What a horror show*, no exclamation point.

These *Inklings* make a bid, a modest bid—modest by my
lights—for your approval, your attention, your respect. Some
of the transitions are too jumpy; perhaps I am caught from
time to time with my probabilities exposed. My prose resem-
bles his, we owe each other much. I know all this. There's no
immortality here, and much that's perishable. But before you
snicker, or purse your lips and shake your head so sadly, answer
me: What would you have made of what's left? First looking
down the hole of a madman's piece week upon week, then
feeling his imagination splash against your eyeglasses, then
getting whacked with the "archives," then . . . be gentle.

I'm at Point No Point. You'd be surprised how little a man
really needs. To get by, I mean. I hang around the Brigadier's
place, and whether or not I'm to be thanked, people have
begun to drift into town to play in the amusement hall. Pinball
is my game, and I'm good at it. The kids watch me play, they
mimic my moves, my sudden pullback before I snap the steel
ball into play, my elbows-out flipper work, my resignation at
the outcome. I even invented a pinball of my own, and the
Brigadier had it wired up for me, he's a prince. I call it LIT.
The player attempts to direct his ball to the *Red Hot Center*.
The lucky winner gets no replay but a flashy jacket blurb from
Samuel Beckett, and a tin Edmund Wilson rises from his coffin
to shake hands with V. Nabokov, and both agree in flashing
violet lights that the player has done himself a BLOCK-
BUSTER and join with Beckett and Bellow and Borges in the
confession that they COULDN'T PUT THE BLAMED
THING DOWN!!! The book goes to the Disney people for
a theme park—seven figures—bells punctuate the deal, Jambo-
ree! In place of tilt, the poor schlump rings up a rejection slip
in funereal Gothic script: OUR LIST IS FULL. Lights out.

The other day I fed eighty of Baby Hughie's dimes into my machine trying for a perfect score, by my lights: pointless. Tried to shoot five balls through the maze of rewards and punishments without ringing a single bell, lighting a single light. I tried and tried, but the best I could achieve were some very low scores, some very dull games.

Maybe the Brigadier will indulge me with another personalized diversion. Replace his beleaguered, shrieking target bear with a representation of me, hit and hurt, lumbering on rails from this wall to that, always with a three-day growth. Glasses? They're not really me, I think. After the publication of *M'n'M* I put them away, I thought for the duration. I felt better without them, unseen rather than unseeing. I felt like I was swimming alone through a benign sea, pretty illusion. I broke them out again, for this. I'm wearing them now.

I haven't given up on Kate, not by a long shot. She's not like the others, she's got staying power, she's a backlist lady. She promised to bring Robin up here a few weeks ago, but she didn't. She promised to send him by bus last weekend, but something came up. I saw the telegram slipped under my door like the last one. I know all about telegrams. There will never be one from Scandinavia asking me to accept honor and money from the munitions dealer. To know this is a relief, I can relax. This telegram said I DON'T KNOW JUPE I WISH IT HADN'T CHANGED BUT IT CHANGED. I understand. But I'll hang on, give her more time. After all, I'm not out of print yet.

Come twilight I walk down to my dock. After so many years of desuetude and neglect the planks have gone rotten, so I pick my way with care around the soft spots. I sit at the end and stare across the swamp grass and mud toward the tideline somewhere out there. I look for a masthead light, and think about my wife and my son, and about this book.

Ships do come in, from time to time. And if one will not come in for me, I'll go find one, and seize it. Two can play the Mole's game. One of the hoodlums who laughed at him, and tormented him, lives near here. Geoffrey Wolff. He has set himself up as a critic, I'm told. The Mole left me his Python. There's one shot left in the Volvo's combustion chambers. I won't settle for pity. I won't. Really. I mean it. I mean what I say. Like the lady said, words count.

About the Author

GEOFFREY WOLFF was educated at Cambridge and at Princeton University, from which he was graduated summa cum laude in 1961. He has taught at Istanbul University, Middlebury College, Goddard College and Princeton. He is the literary critic of *New Times* and has been the book editor of the *Washington Post* and of *Newsweek*. Mr. Wolff's stories and essays have appeared in *Esquire, Atlantic Monthly, American Scholar, Quest, New Republic, New Leader, MORE* and many other periodicals. He has been a Guggenheim Fellow and a Senior Fellow of the National Endowment for the Humanities. He has written two previous novels—*Bad Debts* and *The Sightseer*— as well as a biography of Harry Crosby, *Black Sun.* He lives with his wife and two sons in Vermont's Mad River Valley.